Open Range Fury

Anson Hawkstone is on the trail of an errant husband who deserted his wife and infant child to become a cowboy in Wyoming Territory. But Hawkstone's quest becomes complicated when he encounters three women – a deserted Mormon wife, a white Kiowa captive, and a Chinese girl abandoned by her parents – and ends up escorting them on their wagon journey to Cheyenne. But a range war is about to happen and Hawkstone and the women become caught up in it, leading to an inevitable showdown involving Hawkstone, a ranch foreman, a bounty hunter, and the missing husband.

By the same author

Shadow Shooters

Writing as George Snyder
The Gunman and the Angel
Dry Gulch Outlaws

Open Range Fury

George Arthur

A Black Horse Western

ROBERT HALE

© George Arthur 2018
First published in Great Britain 2018

ISBN 978-0-7198-2776-1

The Crowood Press
The Stable Block
Crowood Lane
Ramsbury
Marlborough
Wiltshire SN8 2HR

www.bhwesterns.com

Robert Hale is an imprint
of The Crowood Press

Typeset by
Derek Doyle & Associates, Shaw Heath
Printed and bound in Great Britain by
4Bind Ltd, Stevenage, SG1 2XT

ONE

In 1877, during a soft spring rain, Anson Hawkstone rode the buckskin mare north of Santa Fe as the trail became rocky and steep. He felt pulled toward Wyoming Territory by the request of his seagoing, world-sailing mate, and had trailed the boy more than a month this far. Before Hawkstone crossed into Colorado, he relived his last conversation with the sea captain, now shipyard owner, Captain Ben Coral.

First, there had been the letter.

Hawkstone carried the letter from Fort McLane to the Apache village where Rachel Cleary, now Rachel Good Squaw, the medicine woman, lived in her small hut, the hut shared with Hawkstone when he was in the area. Rachel and Hawkstone carried personal history, from early days when she was a sixteen-year-old orphan carrying his child. He had been raised from the age of seven by Apache, and did not know about her 'family condition' when he and Ben Coral, both sixteen, went to sea and for eight years sailed in and out of world ports. He returned to San Francisco to find Rachel turned out by the orphanage as a girl of low morals, the baby born dead, and she had been seized by a tribe of Chiricahua Apache and taken to Arizona Territory. After two years, his search for her failed. He married, and while he scouted for the army out of Santa Fe, his family was blown apart during a bank robbery. He never recovered, and once he had butchered those responsible, he turned outlaw and spent three years in Yuma Territorial prison. When released, he returned to his Apache tribe to seek a kind of peace.

It was years later, when shot to pieces and near death, that he was taken to the medicine woman and found his Rachel once again, now forty, living with another Apache tribe near Fort McLane, seeing to their medical needs. She welcomed Hawkstone, and wanted him with her when he could.

While children lined with belly-aches, and coughs, and men came to the medicine woman with gunshot wounds and broken bones, and women sought help with ailments and childbirth, Rachel Good Squaw, the medicine woman, was there. Hawkstone hunted with braves, and alone, to provide the village with meat. He spoke with cavalry officers who, at times, tried to harass villagers, and in a small way his presence protected the little band. She prepared his meals, and at night, when they were alone together in the hut, they read or spoke of their past while they had been apart, and after the lantern was blown out, they held each other.

In this way, they lived their life.

Rachel sat in the pine chair outside her hut and listened while Hawkstone read the letter from his shipmate, Ben Coral. She smoked her clay pipe and nodded at the words. Her flaming red hair sparkled in the setting sun. She wore a buckskin skirt to her knees and calf-high moccasins. She was smooth to touch and soft to hold and had elegant hands. He sat in the chair he had built and placed close to hers, while her hand rested on his arm as he read.

When the letter was finished, she said, 'This means you're gonna leave me. You'll go to San Francisco, to Ben, and you'll chase after this jasper who deserted Ben's daughter and young-un. What was his name, again?'

'Linus Raines. Ben writes the boy took off to cowboy in Wyoming Territory.'

'Just an infant,' Rachel said. 'He took off and left that girl with a tiny baby.' She nodded and inhaled from the pipe and blew smoke, as if she knew the pain of such feelings. 'Yes, you should go.'

Hawkstone studied her face. The blue clay tattoo line ran from her lower lip to just under her chin. Her triangle face still carried high cheek bones and sharp features, except for the full lips.

'I think you'll be glad to see me leave,' he said.

Rachel looked off across the mesa away from the village. 'Yes, I've had enough man cluttering my life, being under-foot. I want you to go.' She turned to him with soft eyes. 'My Viking sailor, that Peacemaker strapped to your hip, with light curly hair and those hazel eyes, big and raw-boned. You do bring your moments for me. You have a way about you, Anson Hawkstone.' She pointed the pipe at him. 'You better not be gone too long. When I start to miss you, the ache is more than I can bear. I crave you deep and serious. Before too long you better get yourself back to me, hear? Now tell me a Ben Franklyn.'

Hawkstone smiled at her. '*The proof of gold is fire, the proof of woman, gold; the proof of man, a woman.*'

For a man used to the open plain, San Francisco appeared cluttered and haphazard, with jerky movement and loud screech, bang, clump noises. Not so at the docks. The docks made sense.

Ship masts swayed with the tide, and an afternoon stiff breeze blew across the bay to assault docks and city alike; the wind blew unchecked, gaining strength across the open Pacific from the shores of Japan.

Hawkstone and Ben Coral sat on the foredeck of an almost complete clipper, the ship still smelling of fresh-cut fir and calking, still on the ways, ready to slide into her element. They drank Jamaican rum that he was reminded poured like syrup and tore at the throat going down.

'She's yours if you want her, Hawkstone,' Ben said. 'A three-master with enough cargo hold and clouds of sail to blow her across any ocean, carrying whatever goods you like. She's the *Distant Star*, and she waits your command.'

Ben Coral was still called 'Captain', though he now owned a shipyard that built clippers. He had earned command coming over the scuppers and pushing up to deck crew, then mate, then captain. His presence demanded respect. Over six feet tall, with a bush of black and grey facial hair, his mahogany eyes were penetrating and his hair surrounded his head. He had huge hands, and a reputation for running a stern but fair ship. He and Anson Hawkstone had shipped aboard another clipper as boys, and in eight years had visited to drink and eat and couple with girls from many of the backwater ports of the world, through the South China Sea to the Chinese coast, to the London docks and Moroccan shores, to the man-spoiling islands of the South Pacific where they sampled innocent maidens eager to please.

'I ain't a man for the sea no more,' Hawkstone said.

Ben leaned forwards. 'Ah, my friend, I can tell by the way you fondle her with your eyes. Your blood needs the mix of sea water mixed in it. You need the motion of a good ship under the soles of your boots.'

Hawkstone slugged down a gulp of the Jamaican rum. 'I got Rachel now. My wandering days are done. I'm only here because of your letter.'

Ben slapped Hawkstone's knee. 'Hell, bring Rachel aboard. Many captains now carry their wives. It would be an adventure unlike any she's ever known.'

'She likes what she's doing.'

'Ah, Anson Hawkstone.' He leaned back. 'I was her favourite, you know? It could have been me got her in a family way them years ago. She liked me better than you.'

8

Hawkstone smiled. 'Hold that thought. She liked you. She went with me.'

'By luck. One word from me, a gesture. Ah, we went to sea as lads and left the poor girl in that way. No excuse for us.'

'I didn't know.'

Ben nodded. 'And how is she now? Did those years with the Apache harden her? Has she lost her fiery softness?'

They sipped rum.

Hawkstone said, 'As a captive girl she went with a brave. Had two sons. Father and sons were slaughtered by the cavalry out of Fort Grant down along the San Pedro River. She moved, became the medicine woman and kept to herself until I found her again.'

'And now you're with her?'

'When I can be. When she can put up with me. She's forty now, Ben, she has little patience for the ways of men.'

'Then she *has* changed.'

'Some. But at times when we're alone together, the girl is still there. She shows herself to me. The woman too. Now and then the woman lets it slip how much she cares. She doesn't mean to. It might be a gesture or a word, but it's there.'

'Only she's done with you now and sent you after my letter.'

'She has. I'm here.'

'First off, Hawkstone, you're not to kill the barnacle slime. You can break his bones and shoot him to pieces, but don't kill him.' He handed Hawkstone a tintype photo of the stiff couple. Linus Raines was not a handsome man. Martha looked better than he thought she might. 'I got plans for the bastard that will be worse than dying, but will end that way.'

Hawkstone studied the photo as he slugged down rum. 'Ben, I didn't even know you got yourself married.'

Ben nodded. 'She was French, from one of the islands off Colombia. She never really took to sea. Having baby Martha

9

almost killed her. Finally, one of them South Pacific diseases done her in, and that was the end of that. I had Martha on my hands and a ship to run. But she took to it good. The girl is a natural born sea gal. I'd hoped when she come of age she'd hook up with a sailor. Didn't matter to me, a seaman, however plain and simple, or how deep in the hold his berth swung. I had money and influence and my ships were sailing the sea. I could'a done something for the lad, brought him up to the deck, made him a mate, even a captain. But, no, she got herself in that San Francisco crowd with money and snobbery, and my little girl fell under the spell of a dandy named Linus Raines, and he insisted Martha call him her "Gypsy Man".'

Ben's lips tightened. He slugged down rum. 'He ain't no man, Hawkstone. First thing, he stays out all night, carousing and spending what ain't his, then he gets my Martha with child. When that ain't enough, he decides to go cowboy in Wyoming Territory. Just up and packs and rides out. I sent men after him, but he's slippery as a snake. I heard he was in Nevada, somewhere's around Virginia City. Then Utah Territory, headed up through Colorado to Wyoming Territory. He's gone now, and I want you to find him and bring him back, not dead, but barely alive won't bother me one bit.'

'What you going to do with him?'

Ben Coral leaned back and studied the glass in his hand. 'What's gonna happen to Raines ain't fit for a man to know or see. Return him to me, and his future is foregone.'

10

TWO

No word reached Hawkstone about Raines through Virginia City and Nevada, nor across Utah Territory, nor at Bent's Fort near La Junta, Colorado, which was more a mountain-man trading post than military fort. Riding into Colorado Territory, sagebrush and greasewood remained but also gave way to tall spruce, aspen, firs and pines, and plenty of rocks. Along the South Platte out of Denver toward the plateau headed toward Nebraska was Pawnee country. Riding his buckskin mare with an old grey pack horse, Hawkstone entered the Pawnee grasslands of Colorado where the Crow river flowed on the right and the Rockies touched clouds on his left. Up north were the Laramie mountains. He shared a campsite with Arbuckle's coffee and beans with a wrangler, Bronco Tex Withers. Bronco Tex had five mares he had been working for two months or more. He had roped them from a mustang herd running along the grasslands and had the mares broke, shod and gentled some.

Bronco Tex looked like a scarecrow in a wheat field. He hadn't shaved in a week. He was dressed in dirty cow-puncher clothes, and when he removed his hat, his forehead shone bright white against his sun-scorched face.

'Gentled some,' he said, looking off where the mustang mares were tied to a cluster of cottonwoods along a creek. 'They can be rid, and mebbe trained to work cows in a few

11

weeks. Ain't no way they'd pull a wagon. Nothing for kids to ride.'

'What you going to do with them?' Hawkstone asked.

'Sell 'em to you, pard. I was gonna drive them to a man named Garth Austin who deals in horses he sells to the army at Fort Laramie. He's up just south of Cheyenne along Orchard Valley.' He sighed deep and closed his eyes. 'I ain't got that kind of riding and herding in me no more.' He pointed to the five mares. 'They's good broncs, hardly buck at all when you swing in the saddle. I'll sell them to you for twenty dollars each. Old Garth will give you fifty or sixty sure.'

'I'm looking for a fella. Not sure I need to do horse trading too.'

'You going that way, just take them along. Let 'em eat the grass and drink creek and river water along the way. They won't be no trouble. You might ride one now and then so they know what they's for. Garth will give you a profit. Who's the fella you looking for?'

Bronco Tex looked at the wedding photo, but had no word on the lad, Linus Raines. Hawkstone gave him the hundred in gold coin. He figured that if Austin didn't buy the mustangs, he'd sell them himself at Fort Laramie, even half broke. The next morning, he pushed them along north.

The mares were a handful. One appaloosa mare had a colt running beside her, a long-legged youngster which frolicked around the old grey mare as if teasing, but didn't stray far from its mother. Besides the appaloosa, there was a reddish-brown bay, a calico pinto, a light dun and a chestnut roan. A group of four Cheyenne followed the mares for a day as though looking for a way to take them. Hawkstone wasn't sure if he'd kill them trying to take his horses, maybe not. They looked starved and pathetic. Farther north had been war with the Dakotas, the Sioux, and added slaughter would continue. Crazy Horse had surrendered, but more soldiers rode towards Fort Laramie every day along the old Oregon Trail up from Kansas and Nebraska. Not near as many used the Trail now the Union Pacific was in, but not all could afford to haul household goods cross-country by rail, so many wagons were still used to roll for Oregon.

Wind from the Rockies carried a bite to it, enough for Hawkstone to keep wearing his buffalo coat. Under it was the leather vest over his green flannel store-bought shirt, and Levi's jeans with copper rivets at the pockets from Fort McLane, not far from Rachel's hut. He kept his flat-brimmed plains Stetson pulled low, and when early spring bitter gusts hit, he tied his kerchief over the hat to his chin. He had stopped wearing spurs when he gave up droving, many years ago. Even then they had been dull, not as sharp as some which left bleeding wounds in the sides of their mounts. The years when he rode through the Brazos of South Texas with its clusters of sharp cactus balls that stuck to everything, he wore thick leather chaps. He had not needed them in Arizona Territory, nor did he up here in the high prairies.

Most trails originated along the banks of rivers. Hawkstone continued to push his small herd along the South Platte along the north-east corner of Colorado. He planned to cut across to the North Platte at the Wyoming border, then into Orchard Valley and maybe connect with Garth Austin. The day was about noon, a Thursday, sunshine blanketed grey from fast-moving clouds racing through passes along the Rockies looking to bring more than a hatful of rain. If the storm got noisy he'd have to hobble the mares, or at least tie them along a string.

But the rain held off as he walked the buckskin behind the tiny herd. They came down off a mesa, and edged along a rocky bluff, Hawkstone looking for shelter. Ahead, farther down towards a feeder creek, he saw a wagon in a clearing, sitting alone without horses. It looked too small to be a

Conestoga, maybe a converted Studebaker bedding packer, about the size of a cattle drive chuck wagon, with the canvas arch top shaking in the cold wind.

'Hello, the wagon,' Hawkstone called as the small herd spread to eat grass. The grey pack horse came up and stood beside the buckskin.

'I got me a scattergun,' a woman said from somewhere behind the wagon.

'Good for you. You won't need it for me. I bring no harm.'

'Says you. Every man wants something.'

Hawkstone shifted in his saddle. 'Name is Anson Hawkstone from down Fort McLane way in Arizona Territory.'

The woman still did not show herself. 'What you doing way up here?'

'Looking for a fella. Mebbe you seen him. Not quite handsome young jasper, dresses kinda dude fancy, just past twenty, lots of hair, clean face, quick to grin, last seen riding a chestnut.'

'Seen nothing like that. I suppose he thinks he's a ladies' man.'

'He does.' Hawkstone stepped the buckskin forward four steps.

'Don't be coming any closer until I say. I hold this scattergun and I know how to use it.'

Hawkstone looked back over his shoulder. 'We got some weather coming, ma'am. If you want me gone, say so, and I'll ride off someplace else.'

She came around to the back of the wagon, still out of sight. The barrel of the single shot poked around the corner above the wagon wheel. 'My husband took our sick horses to get tended to. I want to make sure you ain't here to take advantage of a woman alone. He'll be back quicker than you'll know.'

'Yes'm,' Hawkstone said. 'I'll just move my little herd on out of here and be on my way. I got to settle them down before the rain comes.'

'Wait.' She came out to the side of the wagon with the shotgun still aimed at him. 'You can't just leave a woman alone here.'

She wore grey gingham tight at the waist and bodice and soiled at the hem. Her brown hair was piled in a bun behind her head, with strands wispy around her ears. She looked about thirty, with a pinched face showing a life of trouble.

Hawkstone said, 'I thought your husband was coming right back.'

'We're Mormons, heading to the Oregon Trail, going to start a new life in Oregon Territory.'

'Yes'm. How long he been gone?'

'He lit out day before yesterday.'

Hawkstone sat in his saddle. Nobody had invited him to step down. He reckoned she knew what he was thinking. 'Did he take all your money?'

The aim of the shotgun went down to her shoes. Her lower lip began to quiver. Her shoulders shook. 'Every penny.'

Hawkstone shifted in the saddle. 'Yes'm.'

She looked up at him as if she saw him for the first time. 'Please. Mr Hawkstone. I got brewing coffee, good Arbuckle's. Please step down. Do whatever you got to do with your horses. If you was going to do something to me you'd have done it by now.'

Hawkstone swung to the rocky ground. 'Yes'm.'

She watched while he silently stretched rope for a string line. The mustang mares allowed him to tie them to the string. They began to eat the grass.

He unsaddled the buckskin, and dropped the saddle next to the wagon. 'Mind if I stay under the wagon, ma'am?'

She had pushed the shotgun into the back of the wagon.

15

'Just so you don't think about coming *in* the wagon.'

'No, ma'am.' He began to unpack the grey.

'I'm Ruth Bowers,' she said. 'Mrs Bowers.' She started to stick out her hand but withdrew it. She had green eyes that blinked at him.

'I can get some beans started,' he said. 'I got a little smoked ham left.'

'I got left-over venison.' She followed him to the campfire. 'It's the last. I think he'll come back to me, Mr Hawkstone. He's basically a good man.'

Hawkstone turned to face her. He pushed his palm against the Peacemaker Colt .45 on his right hip. 'First off, Mrs Bowers, you got to stop thinking of him as a man. I don't know what you got in that wagon, but he's moving faster. He's got two horses, one to ride and one to load with supplies bought with the money he took. Whatever he was, whatever he is, it's a lot less than a man. He may be travelling to Oregon Territory, but now he's moving fast and light.'

She stood at attention, staring at him. Her lips were tight. Her eyes turned wet. 'You don't know that. How do you know that?'

'I know men. I've seen them at their best and their worst, all around the world.'

'Do you think *you're* a good man?'

'That ain't our situation here, ma'am. Nothing here is about me. It's about you and what you're going to do.'

'I need horses to pull this wagon. You got horses.'

'They're just broke. They won't hitch up. I got two horses can maybe pull the wagon. Depends what you got in it.'

'Just my things.'

'Uh-huh. Let's have a look-see.'

Without hesitation, Ruth Bowers pulled open the back curtain. Dominating the back half of the wagon was a grey and rusty four-burner cast-iron wood stove. 'It was my great-grandmother's, who has met her maker. It has been in my

16

family for generations. It's a precious heirloom.'

'Send it to her,' Hawkstone said.

'What?'

'You must'a had many words with your worthless husband over that heirloom.'

'Hawkstone, I'll tell you what I told him.'

'No, you won't ma'am. Here's how the buffalo ate the grass. Either that heirloom sits on the ground here next to the creek, or you sit here in the wagon all alone, without moving. Look there, the floor is already starting to crack and sink with the weight. A stretch of bumpy trail and the whole wagon bottom might fall out. You say the word, Ruth Bowers, and I'll leave you all alone with your arm around your family heirloom, happy to be together. Now, that's the way of it.'

THREE

Ruth Bowers complained when the rain came down from the Rockies in sheets. While Hawkstone, wearing his yellow slicker over the buffalo coat, swung the axe at three eight-inch thick pines, she complained over the plight of her family heirloom. The pine logs were cut at fifteen feet. Hawkstone lifted the ends one at a time and dragged them together. When the three were tied at the head and dug in to spread across the base of the wagon, Ruth Bowers complained as Hawkstone peeled back the roof cover and let rain inside the wagon. He dropped the hinged back rail of the wagon. Using a quad-pulley at the head, he tied the biggest rope he had around the stove. With more effort than he liked, he lifted the stove up until, to the sound of creaks and groans and cracks, it cleared the floor of the wagon.

'Aren't you going to hitch the horses?' Ruth asked.

'If I can get to it before the river bank turns to mud, I can mebbe pull it forward eight or nine feet by hand with the wagon tongue. There's a slight incline might ease the roll. You help at one of the wheels.'

'The wheels are muddy.'

'Yes'm. I figure the right rear.' He started for the front of the wagon. 'Don't know how long the stove can dangle there. We better get cracking.'

Wearing just a canvas sheet with a hole for the head against the rain, and a yellow sun bonnet, Ruth shuffled to

18

the right back wheel and gripped the rim. Hawkstone picked up the wagon tongue, and with it held tight against his armpit, he pulled with all his weight. The wagon resisted at first, then with Ruth pushing at the wheel, it moved a foot, two feet, then eight feet, much lighter without the added stove weight.

The rope snapped and the stove fell to the muddy ground with a loud thud, splashing a wave of water around it. The oven door screeched and twisted off.

'You broke it!' Ruth cried.

'Yes'm. Let's get the roof cover back on the wagon.'

Once the cover was on, they spread a ten-by-ten square canvas to the left side from the top. Then they spread another canvas sheet on the ground under it. They sat on the dry canvas, and Hawkstone rolled a Bull Durham and lit it as he studied drainage away from the wagon while the rain hissed. He leaned under the wagon and pulled a bottle of cheap whiskey from his saddle bag. He took a slug and offered the bottle to Ruth.

'Drink of the devil,' she said.

'And saints,' Hawkstone said.

Ruth looked at the bent, broken stove. 'It's going to rust to nothing.'

'The wagon will move easier now.' Hawkstone took another slug and a long drag. He looked at her dress, soaked from the waist down. 'Some women take to cutting enough off a few inches from the bottom of their dress, so it don't drag.'

'Too short, and the wind blows it around and too much shows.'

'I knew one woman sewed lead weights around the hem, kept it in place. Had it cut a few inches above the ankles. Easier to walk, too. How come you ain't got a slicker?'

'Just never got one. I figured I'd spend rainy days and nights in the wagon.'

Hawkstone took a swallow, shaking his head. 'That don't make no sense at all.' He squinted at her. 'How come you Mormons come so far north? I thought you folks settled in Utah Territory, down around Salt Lake. Ain't that where the Mormons hang out?'

'We came from Omaha. Tom was Mormon. I'd been Presbyterian until I met him. Tom is my husband.'

'What took all your money and the horses. And mebbe the slickers, too.'

Her lips tightened and her chin stiffened. 'He had another wife, but he wanted me too. I wouldn't marry him to be wife number two, but she up and died so I thought it was OK. Tom is quite a bit older than me, fifty-seven. I'm twenty-nine.'

Hawkstone shook his head again. He swallowed more whiskey. '*Beauty and folly are old companions.*'

She frowned at him. 'What is that?'

'Sometimes I spout off my version of a Benjamin Franklyn quote, near as I can remember, what I think fits the occasion.'

'Am I the beauty, or the folly?'

Hawkstone kept any response to himself. He said, 'When the rain lets up, I'll hitch my horses and take you to Fort Laramie. I seen many soldiers pass to there, it may be too crowded for civilians. We might have to stop in Cheyenne.'

'Tom told me we should bypass Cheyenne, too rowdy and evil.'

Hawkstone flipped the spent cigarette into the creek. 'Rowdy and evil? Last, I checked, it had a population of about three thousand. Men outnumber women six-to-one. It has twenty-seven saloons, four brewers, eight millionaires, and women have had the vote since about 1870. Selling drinks is the largest service industry. Anybody thinks Cheyenne is rowdy and evil ain't never visited Tombstone, down in Arizona Territory.'

'I suppose, of course, that you have.'

'Yes'm. I used to live there.'

'And you're up here looking for a man?'

'A boy. Ain't no stretch anybody can call him a man.'

The next morning, the grey mare didn't mind getting hitched to the wagon. She went along with just about anything without much fuss. The buckskin, however, wanted nothing to do with such nonsense. She jerked and jumped and kicked out behind, and it took most of an hour to get her to settle. The colt came close to Hawkstone while he hitched the horses, but only to see what he was doing. It never hung around long, and soon went scurrying back to its mother.

Hawkstone wasn't about to let the mares run loose. He had seen too many stray Cheyenne, Sioux and Pawnee hanging about waiting for a chance to run them off. After letting them drink their fill from the creek, he knotted a line from the appaloosa to the back of the wagon, and the other mares he tied neck to tail strung back in a line.

With Ruth Bower sitting beside him, Hawkstone slapped the reins in the air above the horses' backs to get them pulling, and the wagon rolled away from the creek and along the bank trail towards the South Platte river. The rain was gone and had left the air clear as crystal, and cool, until the sun arced towards mid-day. The pack from the grey had been piled inside the wagon, and Hawkstone added his buffalo coat to it – the green flannel shirt and vest were warm enough, and he liked the quicker access to his Peacemaker. Ruth had left the small trunk open, and he saw a photo of her with a man he figured to be Tom, the runaway husband, posed stiff like at a wedding.

The stray Sioux were visible, five of them riding painted ponies. They stayed behind the wagon, but kept closing the gap with the horse string. Their deerskin clothing was ragged, and they carried Winchester rifles across their saddles. Hawkstone doubted they packed much ammunition. He kept his own Winchester '76 leaned against the seat next to him. He had plenty of ammunition.

Ruth saw them too. 'What will you do if they go after the horses?'

'Shoot them dead.'

Since the slaughter of the egomaniac, General Custer, up along the Little Big Horn, a real war had been lodged against all tribes. Crazy Horse had surrendered and been knifed to death in his cell. Other chiefs trickled into forts as their tribes starved. The white man continued to decimate what buffalo still roamed the high plains, so the natives needed to steal cattle. And horses.

Hawkstone had sailed the world in his youth, so he had seen the reality of slavery and conquered people. Both had been around since Man stood and picked up a limb, and would likely be around so long as one man or group saw something he wanted that another man or group possessed. The Europeans came to America and multiplied, and conquered most land and the native people on it. Congress even passed a law declaring the tribes not to be nations, but homeless natives, wards of the government. Indians were a conquered people, and in time would likely fade to oblivion, stuck on their isolated reservations.

Hawkstone neither liked nor disliked what was happening – it was the way of the world. Soft-hearted people who attempted to change life and the native plight were just spitting in the wind. The inevitable moved along with few hiccups. Hawkstone held no personal hatred for Indians, but if they came against him or his, he'd shoot them dead as a rock-flattened desert lizard, as he would any man.

The pinto mare was tied at the rear. The colt ran alongside the string, but kept turning its head back. One of the braves had become bold. He rode right up to the pinto and reached for the rope knot. Hawkstone handed the reins to Ruth and picked up his Winchester. The canvas across the back of the wagon was open so he might see the horses clearly. While one brave fiddled with the knot, another aimed his rifle towards the back of the wagon.

Hawkstone, now in the back, said, 'Bend down flat, Ruth.'

He noticed something different as the second brave fired at the wagon. A rifle shot crack echoed off surrounding hills, and the bullet tore a searing gash in the canvas. Hawkstone shot the brave at the pinto knot first, then quickly racked the lever and shot the second brave before another bullet came. Both braves jerked from their mounts and hit the rocky ground hard. Another brave raised his rifle to his shoulder, but Hawkstone dropped him back over the rump of his pinto.

What he had noticed earlier was that one of them was a girl. She turned her horse to run, while the remaining brave peeled away along the creek. The pintos were a handful and reared and jumped, stirred up by the string of mustangs; the girl was thrown from hers and hit a sharp boulder as big as the wagon. She crawled out of sight while the brave finally got the horses to run in the same direction across the creek. Hawkstone figured the man had no ammunition, so he didn't shoot the brave down. The string of mustangs jumped and snorted against each other. No words would soothe them, so he kept his silence. He climbed forwards and took the reins from Ruth and stopped the wagon. With his Winchester in hand he swung down from the seat.

Ruth had sat again, her shotgun across her arms. 'Where are you going, Mr Hawkstone?'

'That's a white girl, and she's hurt,' Hawkstone said.

FOUR

Left-over rain puddles dotted the creek bank as Hawkstone went back to the girl. She had crawled behind the boulder she hit. He carried the Winchester loose. He watched the forest across the creek where the brave had gone, followed by the pintos. As he walked, he unfastened the leather loop holding the hammer down on the Colt .45, and circled around the rock to the girl. The mustangs still stomped, a high whinny from the colt.

Splashing across the creek at a run, coming at him, the brave looked about mid-teen, with a scowl on his face and a wicked-looking knife in his hand. And he was fast. He ran straight for Hawkstone, letting out a high-pitched scream. Close quarters between rocks didn't allow Hawkstone to swing the Winchester around. He fell back with the brave one step away, pulled the Peacemaker and fired the Colt against the Sioux's belly. The force knocked the boy back. He fell off to the left, blood gushing from his gut. The scream was cut off, but the knife lashed out again, nicking Hawkstone slightly across the left forearm. He fired the .45 again, the bullet hitting the Indian through the temple.

'Please, mister,' the girl said. 'Please, don't shoot me. I didn't do nothing. I wasn't going to steal your horses. Please, just say you ain't going to shoot me.'

Hawkstone holstered the Peacemaker. 'Probably not.

They had you captured.'

She was sitting on the damp ground with her back against the boulder. She was in some pain. 'Yes, sir. I been with them about two years now.'

'Where did you hit?'

She gripped her left knee. 'Below here, my lower leg. It hurts bad.'

She wore a deerskin skirt at her knees and fringed blouse with moccasins just over her calves. She was a slip of a girl, maybe twenty, with thin blonde hair to her shoulder blades and bright blue eyes. She had a tattoo line down each side of her nose. Some might call her pretty in a lost, no-confidence sort of way.

Hawkstone picked up his Winchester and knelt beside her. 'I'll look at that leg. What do they call you, girl?'

'Nettie White Leaf. I'm Nettie White, but that's what they call me. I used to be a school teacher when the Kiowa took me. They traded me to the Sioux for horses. I been with bucks, mister. Ain't had no kids, but I been with them.'

'No need to tell that.' Hawkstone felt the leg below her knee. He tried to be gentle but she grimaced in pain.

'Don't mind me fussing,' she said. 'I'm just a silly girl.'

He smiled. 'Your shin bone is fractured. Not broken through, but I got to set it straight, and tie a splint. It will hurt.'

She blinked her blue eyes until they filmed with tears. Her hands went to tiny fists. 'Do what you got to. What's your name? I should know who's tending me.'

'Hawkstone.'

'That your woman in the wagon?'

'It is not. Ready?'

'Yes, sir.'

She gave out three short screams when he did his business to the leg. He found a limb to tie as a splint.

Ruth Bowers stared from beside the wagon while Hawkstone lifted Nettie White inside and made her comfortable.

'Oh, no you don't. No, sir. You're not putting some buck's whore inside my wagon. She's captured white. Not in my wagon. You know what happens to them.'

Nettie had already started pushing to crawl back out.

Hawkstone shoved her back in. 'You rest easy, Nettie. We got to let that leg heal.'

'Mr Hawkstone,' Ruth said.

Still standing outside the wagon, Hawkstone spun to her and stared. 'Hush yourself, woman. We're going to look after Nettie and let that leg heal. Nothing more will be said.'

'It's *my* wagon.'

'You want me to take my horses and ride along? I can put Nettie on one of the mustangs.'

Nettie put her hand on Hawkstone's lightly nicked arm. 'Please, sir. I don't want to be no trouble.'

'No trouble,' he said. 'You met Ruth Bowers. Her Mormon husband run off with horses and money. I'm taking this here wagon to Cheyenne or Fort Laramie.' He looked at the sky around him. 'We got two more hours of daylight and still three or four days to go.' He looked from one woman to the other. The rainstorm had added little beauty to Ruth. Her brown hair spider-webbed around her head and neck, needing a brush. Her clothing wanted washing. A scowl remained on her face. Nettie was eight or nine years younger but looked fresh and brighter by contrast. Like most hatred, Ruth's prejudice towards captured women had been planted in her by others.

'I don't like this,' Ruth said.

Before Hawkstone turned to the rocks, he pointed a finger at her. '*Whatever begins in anger, ends in shame.*'

*

26

After another night on the trail, a night with Nettie in pain in the wagon, Hawkstone took stock of what supplies they had.

'We're about gone with meat,' he said. 'We'll have to take a day off from the trail so I can hunt some. I'll need my horses.'

Ruth set two sacks aside. 'I got salt and flour, and some molasses. Plenty of Arbuckle's coffee beans. Oats for oatmeal. Bread and oatmeal and coffee is about it.'

Hawkstone began to unhitch the buckskin and grey. He looked up towards the Rockies. 'I'll try to get an antelope. No chance of any wild pigs around. I should be back before dark.'

'We'll have coffee waiting,' Ruth said.

He left the mustangs tied to the wagon on long lines so they might still eat grass. With the buckskin saddled, he hitched the pack frame to the grey. When he mounted, he fixed Ruth with a stare. 'You going to behave yourself?'

Ruth shaded her eyes from the sun with her hand. 'You think I drove my husband away.'

Hawkstone stayed quiet as he rode out of the camp. Whatever he thought he intended to keep to himself.

Hawkstone dropped the antelope with one shot from the Winchester. It was a young buck, lean and quick and full of flight, but would be tasty frying meat. He intended to gut and partially dress the animal before he loaded it on the grey.

But as he pulled his ten-inch bowie, he spotted the scalped body of a man off in a clump of mesquite. The body was naked and covered in knife stabs, but there were enough features in the face for Hawkstone to recognize the stiff-posed man in the wedding picture: Tom, the runaway husband. No horses, of course. It might have been the band who had come after the horses, in which case Nettie White

27

Leaf would know about it. Or another band altogether. Whoever it was, he had to decide if or when he should tell Ruth Bowers. He decided the later the better – maybe when they got to Cheyenne, he'd tell her she was truly on her own.

For now, he had to bury the body.

FIVE

At sundown, Hawkstone was two miles out aimed for the wagon camp. The grey carried the dressed antelope. With fish, once they reached the South Platte, there should be enough eating until Cheyenne and maybe Fort Laramie, even for three. Flour, sugar, salt, more coffee would have to be store-bought in civilization. Folks could no longer just live off the land any more; they were too pampered with the trappings of easy living.

He felt a want for Bull Durham and corn-husk paper for smokes. And whiskey, he was down to his last bottle. He'd have to pace himself.

He missed Rachel and her hut, and the softness of her against him on the bed. Sometimes she kissed him for no good reason. What kind of woman did that? She looked at him with loving eyes and kissed him as if the riverboat was sinking. When he asked why, she told him because he looked like he needed a kiss. And on the bed, she often wrapped her arms around his neck and let her bright red hair spread across his chest. He missed that, too. There was much to miss about Rachel.

A girl came walking towards him out of the darkness. She strode in dainty small steps, walked along the road around a jagged hill into the last remnants of sunlight, and when she saw him she stopped and stared. She had a cloth bundle tied to a cane-sized tree limb balanced on her shoulder. She did not turn and run, which was what he expected: she stood still and watched him, and the meat packed on the grey behind him.

She was Chinese, maybe seventeen or eighteen, and her black hair was in a single braid straight down to her waist, but she had pulled the braid around her neck so it hung down in front of her shoulder. The grey Chinese dress, over her slim boyish frame, hugged her hips and buttoned down the front all the way to her ankles with two-bit-size buttons. Her face was round as the moon and shone, with full lips and almond eyes. Atop her head she wore a wide-brimmed, flat-topped black hat.

'Do you talk American?' Hawkstone asked as he approached her. He reined in the buckskin.

'Are you with wagon train?' she said. 'Do you hunt for a train to Oregon?'

A question with a question. 'The name is Hawkstone. I'm pulling a wagon to Cheyenne with two women aboard. Mebbe they'll be headed for Oregon eventually.'

She squinted at him. 'And you?'

'I'm looking for a fella.'

'Me too. My man go astray. My family push me away from them.' Tears filled her slanted eyes. 'They deserted me for my shame. I am Yin Chun, and I am lost.'

Hawkstone hooked his boot across the saddle horn. He pulled his pouch of Bull Durham from his vest pocket. 'You got no idea where you are?'

'I look for the Oregon Trail.'

'The Trail is easy to find, but it's wide and long, and I don't think you can just walk it with a bundle on a stick.'

'He will find me. He must because of the shame he has done. Or I will find him and we will be together again, me and my Gypsy Man.'

Hawkstone let his crossed leg drop back to the stirrup.

The rolled cigarette stayed in his fingers waiting for a match. 'Did you call him your Gypsy Man?'

She nodded. 'He got me in a family way and now we must find each other. I have been deserted by my family, but we will find them along the Trail. They take our wagon to Oregon where Mama and Papa and my two brothers will open a restaurant.'

Hawkstone sat stiff. 'Yin Chun, you better come along with me. If your Gypsy Man is a fella named Linus Raines, you and me better stick together 'cause we're looking for the same bucko.'

She stepped to the buckskin. 'You know him?'

'Nope, but I intend to. And I got plans for him. You climb on behind me. Stick your tree-limb bundle down there next to the rifle.'

Yin Chun quickly unbuttoned the dress from ankle to the knees then lifted her bare leg enough to step into the stirrup. Hawkstone gripped her arm and swung her up behind him. As the buckskin stepped forwards, he said, 'Looks like you could use something to eat, little one.'

'Yes,' she said. 'I can see you are a good hunter. A mighty hunter.'

'Yes'm. I probably am,' Hawkstone said. 'Among other things.'

Hawkstone unsaddled the buckskin, then watered and fed the horses. The mustangs were still restless because of the gun shooting, but they had settled after a trip to the creek.

Not Ruth Bowers, however. She stomped twenty steps away from the wagon, then spun on Hawkstone, her face flushed. 'This is the final insult, Mister. Now you got some chink Chinee child among us. And you say her family kicked her out? It's obvious what's wrong with her. She must be three, four months along. You're adding her bouncing bundle to our group too?'

31

'I got a feeling the boy I'm looking for is responsible,' Hawkstone said. 'Yin Chun will be with us a while.'

At the wagon, Yin Chun had started carving up the meat. She searched for and found the pots and pans she needed. She had coffee perking on the campfire, and water for tea she had pulled from her limb bundle, and for rice. Inside the wagon with the cover corner raised, Nettie watched.

Ruth said, 'What happens when Tom comes back with the horses? I know he'll be back. What will he think about this circus you brought down on us?'

Hawkstone wrestled in his mind what to tell Ruth Bowers. He had figured to soften the presence of Yin Chun first, get her used to the idea, before giving her the devastating news. 'You meet up and do some talk with the girl. She can help and she knows her way around a campfire. Settle yourself and get along, woman, because tomorrow we'll start moving faster along the trail.'

While Ruth appeared to make an effort toward civility to the Chinese girl, they prepared antelope and beans together for the late meal.

Hawkstone lifted Nettie out of the wagon. She didn't weigh no more than a pillow. He showed her the limb crutch he had cobbled together to help her get around. Though she didn't complain, the pain she felt showed plain on her young face with the tattoo blue-clay ink lines along each side of her nose.

'Set yourself over on this juniper log. I'll check that wrap.' Hawkstone thought maybe he had wrapped the leg fracture too tight. When he removed the bandaging, the leg looked discolored with bruising, but the skin was tight around the wound. He rewrapped it less tight, and tied the limb splint with thin line.

With her crutch, Nettie was no longer restricted to the wagon. She hobbled to the edge of the creek and sat on the edge of a boulder and washed her face and hands. She watched Ruth and Yin Chun fill a plate and hand it to Hawkstone. Even Hawkstone was surprised when Ruth took a filled plate to Nettie and silently handed it to her.

Yin Chun brought Hawkstone a cup of tea. 'You drink tea, it heals many things.' She went back to the campfire and helped herself to a plate of food.

They ate in silence. Nothing was said by the ladies about Hawkstone's hunting success: he was the man, it was expected. After the meal, Yin Chun set to cleaning up. Hawkstone watched the three women while he smoked by the creek. He'd wait until he bedded down on the saddle under the wagon before a last night-time sip of whiskey.

Nettie and Yin Chun sat together on rocks and asked about each other – places, family, trails and incidents in their lives. Both lived lives interesting to the other. With coffee for Nettie and tea for Yin Chun, they spoke low with their heads together.

Hawkstone took Ruth's arm. 'Let's walk upstream a bit.'

Ruth frowned at him. 'What for?'

'I got something to tell you.'

Ruth had fixed up herself while Hawkstone was meat hunting. She might even have bathed in the creek. Her brown hair was clean and in a fresh tight bun. Apparently her small trunk in the wagon carried at least one other dress, dark green with a tight waist. Her face still appeared pinched, and there were few laugh lines around her nut-brown eyes, but with a full meal, she seemed less tense, despite the added slender Chinese girl.

As they walked, picking their way in moonlight along creek bank rocks, he dropped his hand from her arm.

Ruth said, 'Do you have a wife, Mr Hawkstone?'

'I have a woman, the medicine woman.'

'She's a doctor?'

'To the tribe she lives with, she is. To me, she is Rachel.

We've known each other time-to-time since she was sixteen, me eighteen.'

'I wish I had known Tom that long.'

Hawkstone stopped. 'Ruth, I got to tell you about Tom.'

'You mean you don't think he's coming back, that he really did desert me?'

'Don't know if he would have or not. He ain't coming back now, though.'

She turned to face him. 'What are you saying?'

'I found Tom scalped and butchered where the high prairie pushes along foothill rocks. I buried him under rocks along a string of pines.'

SIX

Linus Raines sat on the bench alone in the bunkhouse and sipped coffee. He felt he had stumbled into a sweet way of life. He worked with eight other young buckaroos on a ranch running more than five thousand head. Millie Kyle, owner of the Circle-D, was in her sixties and thought Linus was a nice boy, not much of a cowboy but a fast learner. More important, Millie had a daughter, Lindsey, a skinny twenty-two-year-old who was already calling Linus her 'Gypsy Man'. In less than another week, Linus intended to start fingering the pretty girl's petticoat. The kissing and fondling had already started. As a bonus, there was a group of six nester farms spread along the north end of the valley. Two of the Circle-D buckaroos, Al and Joe Coslet, had already sidled next to a couple of girls and were enjoying themselves three nights a week. The nesters seemed to procreate daughters more than sons. At least three looked past fifteen and ripe for his brand of charm, ready to gather him close as their Gypsy Man.

Besides the Circle-D, the neighbour ranch, the Bar-X, almost five thousand head, competed for water and grazing prairie. Linus sensed conflict, not only between neighbours but between the two ranches and the nesters. Millie was a tough old hide herself, but she couldn't touch the meanness of the Bar-X foreman, a hombre called Ward Cameron. The situation got confusing then for Linus. Cameron was the foreman, but the ranch was actually run by the owner's daughter, Caroline Shelby, twenty-five and a petite, good-looking package with long blonde hair and a high, squeaky voice that never commanded respect. The two times Linus met her she wore buckskin pants. That made him dismiss her for romance. Linus thought buckskin pants were masculine and had no place covering the soft curves of a girl or woman. She belonged in a dress with her smooth firm throat showing, and maybe a bit of mound. He sipped his coffee and pondered if Ward Cameron helped himself to Caroline Shelby sugar. Probably. Caroline's daddy, Trenton, dictated to the Bar-X from back east someplace, confident Cameron could handle anything his shrill daughter couldn't, and, no doubt, her.

The new-fangled barbed wire had been available only three years, but hundreds of miles of it had been strung. In the valley, the range had always been open. Millie threatened fences if Caroline didn't stop hogging the water and didn't keep her cows on her side of the property. But, Lindsey told Linus, it was the nesters who first strung wire to keep cattle out of their gardens and crops, and away from their home buildings. Nobody who had been across open range on cattle drives liked the fences. Many drifters and Texas longhorn drovers had no hesitation in cutting them wherever they stretched. But once the nesters started with wire, they sent it out into range land, and that made the Bar-X and Circle-D also use wire.

Coming across Nevada and Colorado, when he wasn't outrunning Daddies with shotguns trying to make him do right by their daughters, Linus heard of and saw the wire. He never became excited about it. He was from San Francisco society, a fringe hanger-on, without substance to be sure, but at that time his name connected with the daughter of Captain Ben Coral gave him a certain respect. But he wanted to cowboy in Wyoming Territory, and a wife and infant tied him down: the only solution had been to move on. The cute wife would get over it, as Linus would, as soon as he shed the spray of the bay from his heels.

But even a squeaky woman like Caroline Shelby might be too sharp for him. He had to stick with the younger girls. Once they grew to the same twenty-three or so as him, they saw right through him and doubted his sincerity, and the honesty of his patter. He'd had the same problem with his wife, Martha, out there in San Francisco, a place he'd likely never see again. If he hadn't got her in a family way, there wouldn't have been any wedding. He couldn't go back to Nevada, either, as the warrant was still outstanding for shooting that little girl's daddy. He'd come after Linus with a nasty looking double-barrel shotgun, and even though the girl had cried how much she loved her Gypsy Man, Daddy had unloaded both barrels and Linus had had to shoot the man down with his Remington revolver – what was that girl's name? It escaped him – the $500 poster for the killing hadn't travelled as far as Wyoming Territory or Cheyenne, and likely wouldn't reach the Circle-D before he'd had his fill of sweet Lindsey Kyle and moved on to other ranches in the Territory.

Linus Raines put down his empty cup and strode outside the bunkhouse to a fine, sunny spring morning. He was supposed to move a hundred head to the east pasture, then help Al and Joe Coslet check fences along nester lines. He didn't want to do that. When he saw Millie drive the one-horse buggy away towards the settlement, he decided to visit Lindsey and see if he might still catch her in bed in her slippery, warm night clothes.

Linus stood dressed in front of the bedroom mirror. He heard Lindsey stir on the bed behind him. He wished he was taller. Captain Ben hadn't wanted him as a husband for his

Martha because he said Linus was such a little man. A fella might take that several ways. He dressed in a grey suit with silk vest and new cowboy boots. His Remington was cross-draw. Though he didn't consider himself fast as a gunfighter, he might hold his own in a small-town saloon draw. He squinted at himself in the mirror, wearing his mean face. His wife, Martha, had told him his best feature was his boyish good-looks, and he agreed, though not many others did. But he liked his dark facial tone, his long straight nose, and especially his bushy black eyebrows, which he thought made him look mysterious to girls. He pushed his face close to the mirror – on occasion he even touched up the eyebrows with a fingertip of burned black wood. The girls did like a dark mysterious stranger, even if he wasn't especially handsome, or tall. Boot heels helped. He might put something inside the boots to elevate his stature.

From the bed, Lindsey said, 'Come back to me, Gypsy Man.'

He turned and looked for his plains hat. 'I got to go to work.'

'Not yet.' She wore a flimsy turquoise nightgown.

Lindsey Kyle was twenty-two, and besides her beauty, her most outstanding feature for Linus was that her mother, Millie, owned the ranch. When Lindsey was fourteen and spoiled rotten, her father had got kicked to death by a stallion. She had got over it, but nobody had spoiled her like Daddy. She had no interest in ranch life, except for the luxury and comfort it provided. She had been wild in college, and had been kicked out of three. With soft, warm brown eyes and rich blonde hair full to her shoulders, she looked stunning, and generally had her way teasing men. Linus knew this twenty minutes after meeting her. She wanted travel, not ranch life. Linus had decided that was a good idea, and he toyed with keeping her next to him for a spell. Lindsey had the ability to provide him with the spoiled

38

rich life he had never quite reached in San Francisco, but very much wanted to become accustomed to.

Linus looked at her sitting in the middle of the bed. 'You are one good-looking woman, Lindsey Kyle.'

She pouted her lower lip. 'Perhaps. Not good-looking enough to keep you here.'

Linus picked up his hat. 'I told you, I got work.'

Lindsey pulled the nightgown slowly up her legs. 'Wouldn't you rather do something else?'

'You bet.' With his hat on, he checked his Remington and bent to kiss her.

She tried to grab him but he pulled away. She moved up to her knees and wrapped her arms around his neck. 'I'm not done with you.'

He kissed and fondled her, and pushed her away. 'I'll be back. Where did Millie go? To the settlement?'

'Cheyenne. Bankers. They keep pushing at her to sell this ranch.' She sighed. 'I think the bankers intend to own this whole valley. They been talking to the Bar-X, and I hear even to some of them dirt farm nesters. Mostly, they want the cattle we breed for Europe.'

'With it all together, how much acreage we talking?'

'Three hundred and fifty thousand acres. Most of it open range. And more nesters coming. More fences going up. It sweeps all the way up to the foothills.'

At the door, Linus turned for a smile at her. He winked. 'This ranch will bring in a lot of money, Lindsey.'

Lindsey gave him a wicked grin. 'Think what we can do with it all, my Gypsy Man.'

SEVEN

Anson Hawkstone heard bad news when he drove the wagon of women into the Orchard Valley and began his search for Garth Austin, the wrangler who was to buy the mustangs. Austin's horse station had been raided by Lakota Sioux, who had killed everyone there, burned it to the ground, and run off with all the horses.

Hawkstone would have to sell his mustangs in Cheyenne.

He found an overland stagecoach station just outside the valley, which sold him two forty-dollar mules for the wagon. The mules had been pulling the wagon of a honeymoon couple from Missouri who had given up on future dreams, the Oregon Trail, the marriage, and each other. Hawkstone found the mules to be strong and tireless. With his pack in the wagon, he let the old grey run free. He rode the buckskin and herded the mustangs and tried to keep them close to the trail and the wagon. In Cheyenne, he would let the three women find their own way.

Cattle still moved along several trails north from Texas through New Mexico Territory, Indian Territory, Nebraska, and across Colorado and Wyoming Territories to various stockyards, including those just outside Cheyenne. There, the Union Pacific took them east. Hawkstone hadn't driven cattle in twelve years, not since after the war. He rode into the town outskirts inhaling familiar stockyard smells and sounds, and trail-tired cowboy bones at the end of a drive, and it brought back rich memories. But he wouldn't have taken a thousand dollars for the experience, and he wouldn't have paid a nickel for another just like it.

He led the way to a small stable close to the many stockyards that stretched along railroad tracks. In the mid-afternoon, the spring sunshine kept air cool. Fluffy skies drifted from the Rockies. The sign above the living-shack stated 'Footless Stables', and was surrounded by barns and corrals.

'Yup, that's me,' the grizzled man said. He came hopping on a crutch, without his foot, his head and face an explosion of thick pepper hair, explaining: 'I crawled off the Gettysburg battlefield but left my foot behind.' He stared at Hawkstone, then the wagon, then swept his gaze over the mustangs, then looked back at Hawkstone. 'You was in the war?'

'Who wasn't?'

In presence of other horses, the mares snorted at the dust they kicked up.

Footless nodded at them. 'Need a place to keep them for a spell?'

'A day or two. How much?'

'Two dollars a day each.'

'That's pretty hard. I'm looking to sell them.'

'We got plenty of horses here in Cheyenne. You might take them down to Fort Laramie. I hear the army is always looking. But you might get more for them at one of the ranches 'tween here and there, up around Big Horn and Powder River Basin, out through the Green River Valley.'

'I got to provision first,' Hawkstone said. After he herded the mustangs into a small corral, he walked the buckskin to the wagon where the three women sat on the seat watching him.

Footless said, 'Couple of decent size ranches northwest of here, close to Medicine Bow and the Lodgepole River. You might try the Bar-X or Circle-D out that way.'

Hawkstone pulled the wedding photo of Linus Raines

41

from his vest pocket and stretched it out to Footless. 'Ever see a jasper looking like this in town?'

Footless scratched his beard. He rubbed his mouth and squinted up as he handed the photo back. 'Can't say I have. Lot of drifters flow through town. We got fifty vigilante deputies, plus the town marshal and his four deputies, plus the Laramie County Sheriff and who the hell knows how many of his deputies. Mebbe one of them saw the fella.'

'Why so much law?'

'Cattle drives and wild drovers. They do raise some hell, and the bankers and merchants and church folk intend for Cheyenne to stay civilized and capital of the territory. They figure Wyoming will be a state any day now.'

Hawkstone looked down the main street. 'Mebbe we out west here are getting too civilized.'

'You one of them Mormon fellas?'

'No.'

'I only ask on account of your women. I'd invite you in. The missus has a pitcher of sweet buttermilk, only I can't when you got a captured white and a chink Chinee girl expecting.' He focused on Ruth Bowers. 'You the wife?'

'I'm the Mormon,' Ruth said. 'Keep your buttermilk, we'll be headed for town.'

In a main street café, Hawkstone bought the women a beef stew meal. Downtown was crowded with single riders and wagons and prairie schooners pushing towards the Oregon Trail. The Union Pacific train station hummed with voices – little girls loved to scream and run, parents chased them – the platform crowded with travellers toting carpet bags, and gunfighters with tied-down holsters.

After the stew, Hawkstone said, 'I'll get you a hotel room so you can take a bath. I can't afford a room for each of you so you'll have to bunk in together.'

Ruth stared at him with a film of tears covering her nut-brown eyes. 'What will become of us, Mr Hawkstone? I can wire my parents for money back in St Louis, but that may take a week or more.'

'What do you want to do?'

'We talk,' Yin Chun said. 'I want to find my Gypsy Man, but I think now that may not be so.'

Nettie said, 'I got nobody and no place to go.'

Hawkstone put his hand on Ruth's. 'I can front you some gold pieces. I ain't got a lot, but I don't need a lot. I'll have more once I sell the mustangs. You can provision the wagon.'

'The Oregon Trail,' Ruth said.

'To Oregon,' Yin Chun said.

Nettie nodded. 'A new life.'

Ruth patted Hawkstone's hand. 'We want to come with you. We'll rest in the hotel, get a bath, provision, then we'll go with you to sell the mustangs and you can get us on the Oregon Trail.'

'Then you'll be shed of us,' Nettie said.

With the women in the hotel, Hawkstone bought the things he needed for the grey horse's pack, then stopped in *The Green Elephant* saloon to wet his throat. He stood at the crowded bar with his boot on the brass rail listening to men harass five underdressed soiled doves trying to bargain the price of a poke. None of the girls looked past sixteen. The whiskey was two bits a glass and cut with something, maybe kerosene.

A dandy stepped up to him. He wore a derby and had a wide thick moustache and black garters on his arms. He hooked thumbs in the armpits of his black silk vest and grinned. One eyetooth was made of gold.

'You come to town with three women in the wagon, am I right?'

'Something you want?'

'Name is Strong. William Black Strong. I own *The Green Elephant.*' He slapped a hand on the bar. 'Bruno! Get us some decent whiskey over here.'

A man who might have passed for a gorilla brought a fancy etched bottle of bourbon and two fresh glasses and set them on the bar. He ignored Strong and went back along the bar.

Strong poured. 'Send that down your throat, mister, it'll feel like a woman's caress. I want to talk to you about them three girls you got. Well, the one woman and two girls.'

Hawkstone left the glass untouched. 'Nothing to talk about.'

'One girl is a white captive.'

'So?'

'The other – the adorable China doll – is in the family way. We can take care of that. We got a doc in town who specializes in taking care of them problems. Helps our girls here all the time.'

Hawkstone said, 'I think mebbe you better nail a board across your mouth.'

'Now, no need to get hostile. What you say your name was?'

'Didn't say.'

'The third woman, the older white one, ain't pretty or nothing like that, but she's got a decent body, and she sure ain't the ugliest bitch to get a dollar poke. I can put her in here with the girls, she'd cater to the older gentleman trade. The other two we can put in a tent. The China doll, once she's taken care of, got her belly whittled down, we can make special. Get her in a silk hugging dress she might fetch three or even five dollars a poke. I want to buy them, mister. Give you hard gold coin. They can have a real future right here in downtown Cheyenne.'

Hawkstone threw the full glass of whiskey in Strong's face, then punched him into the gold eyetooth, breaking it at the root, and slipped out a side door of *The Green Elephant* before a ruckus started.

44

EIGHT

Linus Raines rode his sorrel next to the long prairie nester fence. A new section had been added, closing off more open range. The afternoon sun began to dip behind the Rockies. He heard the far-off whistle of the train. Folks moving on. He'd have to be moving on now too, as the 'Wanted' poster had reached Cheyenne and was up to a thousand dollars. Al and Joe Coslet were good pards. They told him about the new poster they saw without asking questions. It wasn't like Linus was the only ranch hand to have a poster out on him. Only now the poster wasn't about a killing: it stated, murder. How was he supposed to know the girl was a wife? She looked thirteen, with an innocent child pillow-face and a blossoming body. She turned out to be older than thirteen with a house to keep and a husband to satisfy. The husband creased a .45 slug across Linus' side before Linus stabbed his belly with the eight-inch bowie he always carried in his right boot, then dropped him with the Remington. That was in Colorado Territory just outside Fort Collins.

Now with the Coslet brothers headed back to the ranch, Linus walked the sorrel to meet a sod buster's daughter of fifteen, Janey-Jean Trevor. Her daddy, Miles Trevor, was the leader of all the nesters. He got them stirred up and talked too much about rights, and stuff that didn't interest Linus at all. Besides Janey-Jean, the sod buster leader had two other daughters too young to fool with, and a boy, Earl, of seventeen who didn't like Linus one bit. Linus had already whipped the boy once, without even reaching for the bowie, and was ready to do it again if Earl didn't leave him and Janey-Jean alone so they could fool around.

She came running to him along the hollow that extended from a trickle creek far beyond fences and buildings and other people. Wearing only her calico dress, and her buck tooth smile, she was always so eager, brought on by innocence and hormones and not much education. She was actually dumb as a fence post. What Linus enjoyed was her willowy presence and ready excited attitude. He truly admired her attitude.

On the tall grass next to the creek, Linus had barely got started with Janey-Jean when Earl came riding hard on a plow horse with no saddle. He carried an ancient revolver in his pants waistband. When he saw them, he slid from the horse and drew the weapon. His young face showed he had passed the time he should start shaving. He was a pile of twigs and sticks covered in torn pants too big with suspenders over a worn flannel shirt, and no shoes. His straw hair hung straight to his shoulders.

With the revolver aimed at Linus, Earl looked at Janey-Jean, just pulling down her dress hem. 'Get yourself home.'

'Go away from here, Earl,' she told him. 'This ain't none of your business.'

'You want me to tell Pa?'

'Go ahead.' She stood straight, and with a toss of her young head threw her long brunette hair back over her shoulder to fall to her waist. 'We're in love.'

'You tell him, sweetie,' Linus said. He thought about the bowie to keep down noise, but then figured, no killing might be needed for a righteous brother.

Earl shook his head. He glared at his sister. 'If you don't start for home right now, I'll shoot the bastard in the belly.'

He cocked the hammer back. 'I'll gut him right here and now.'

'Whoa,' Linus said. 'No need to get violent, Earl. I ain't the violent kind. I got a gentler nature.'

'You think you're a lover?'

Linus blinked. 'Why, as a matter of fact I do.'

'I heard about you. You're foolin' with Lindsey Kyle, over to the big ranch.'

'Now that's a lie, Earl. I ain't had nothing to do with Lindsey in more'n a month.'

'And there's a girl down to the Petri farm.'

'Where you hearing all these lies, Earl?'

Janey-Jean moved to stand in front of Linus. 'They *are* lies, ain't they, my Gypsy Man?'

'You know they are, sweetie.' He made a move to gather her in his arms.

Earl grabbed Janey-Jean's arm and yanked her away. 'Get marching, girl. Get yourself home.'

Linus said, 'You go on home, sweetie. We'll have plenty of time to get together.'

'When?' she asked.

'Tomorrow or the next night. I don't want to say with Earl standing here.'

'Oh. OK, you'll get word to me?'

'Absolutely. We got love, don't we?'

'You better know it, my Gypsy Man. Nobody else calls you that, do they?'

Linus grinned at her. 'Only the love of my life.'

'Get going,' Earl said.

Janey-Jean yanked the reins out of Earl's hands. 'I'm taking the horse. You can walk.'

'Here, I'll help you up,' Linus said. He helped her on to the bare back with his hands in places that made her giggle.

Janey-Jean heeled the plow horse and galloped over the hollow and out of sight.

47

Linus waited until he no longer heard the hoofs pounding on prairie. He looked at Earl, who still had the weapon aimed at him. 'Put that thing away, Earl. I cleaned your plow once before and I can do it again.'

'Stay away from my sister. She's too young.'

'Get them young, and they're dumb enough to believe. And, you get that ripening body.'

Earl took a step forwards. 'I oughta blast you right here.'

'You ain't got the sand for it, boy, if that relic will even fire.' Linus pulled the makings for a smoke. 'Earl, you want me to leave her alone, I'll leave her alone.'

'You're still with Lindsey Kyle, ain't you.'

'You look at the ranch and her money, and you tell me what you think.'

'What do you want with my sister?'

'A little diversion.'

'Stay away from her.'

'Have a smoke.'

'Will you keep off our place?'

'Whatever you want, Earl, just put that hogleg away and have a smoke.'

Earl paused. He sighed, and looked down at the revolver. He acted embarrassed to be standing in coming darkness with a gun in his hand. 'She's too young for the likes of you, Raines.'

'I know that now, Earl, on account of you just told me and made me realize. Here.' He handed Earl the makings.

To free his hands, Earl stuck the weapon back in his waistband. He took the paper and sprinkled tobacco from the Bull Durham pouch, then looked at the cigarette.

Linus Raines quickly pulled his Remington and shot Earl twice in the chest. When the boy fell back and went down, Linus shot him again through the head. The gunshots echoed off the dark Rocky Mountains.

NINE

Hawkstone herded the mustangs along the wire fence until he'd had enough. The wagon stopped and the three women watched him dismount and rifle through the pack in the back. He came out with wire cutters and snapped the two strands. The sound of the strands parting echoed across open prairie in the late afternoon. He returned the cutters and mounted.

'Ain't that illegal?' Nettie asked him.

'That fence is illegal. This is open range. No ranch got a right to fence it off. There's sweet grass over there and my mares are hungry for it.' He rode through the cut. The wagon followed. He squinted across green grass towards the setting sun. 'Looks like buildings a far piece over there. We'd have to ride five miles around the fence. I figure we'll camp here. Looks like a creek down off the rise. In the morning, I'll take the mustangs over there to the Bar-X, see what they'll pay.'

While the women prepared the meal, Hawkstone watered the horses. Then he tied them to the wagon with long ropes so they reached the grass. By then fried antelope and beans and rice were ready. Hawkstone sat on the canvas alongside the wagon with his plate.

Yin Chun pointed a finger with a stern look for Hawkstone. 'Drink your tea.'

Ruth slid next to him. 'I'll have money in three more

days. I can pay you back.'

Her face looked more relaxed. The hair bun was tight and neat, and she had bought herself a new yellow dress. The news of her husband, Tom, hadn't hit her as hard as Hawkstone thought it might. The marriage can't have been a happy one. He reckoned Tom hadn't been much of a man.

Nettie hobbled over to the canvas on her crutch. She set her plate down, then eased beside it and smiled at them. She looked very young and pretty except for the tattoo line down each side of her nose. Hawkstone knew of the blue clay ink used by Indians. It was as permanent as skin.

Yin Chun removed the pot from the fire and set it on rocks next to it. She picked up her plate and joined them. She leaned to look at Hawkstone. 'What you do when you sell horses?'

'Find the boy I'm looking for.'

'And then?'

'Take him to his fate back in San Francisco.'

The women looked at each other. Ruth said, 'Can we convince you to come with us?'

'To Oregon? I could swing that way, but I ain't.'

Ruth said, 'Because of the wife deserter?'

'I ain't allowed to kill him. He'll be a handful.'

Ruth cleaned her plate. 'And you're anxious to get back to your tribe, the medicine woman.'

'I am.'

Yin Chun said, 'We'll be on our own.'

Hawkstone cleaned his plate and set it aside. He sipped his tea. He reached in his vest pocket for the makings. 'What you gals ought to do is hook up on a wagon train passing through. Latch on to one coming out of Cheyenne or Fort Laramie. That way you'll have some protection. You should get to Oregon before Yin's baby comes.'

The women were silent for a spell. Then Ruth said, 'A good man is hard to find.'

Hawkstone said, 'Stick together. And remember what my good sidekick, Ben Franklyn, said, '*A jasper may be too cunning for one, but not for all.*'

The ranch hands hit the camp in the shine of the moon just past midnight.

Seven of them rode in making noise. They fired their six-shooters, rode their horses over the camp ashes, lassoed the mules and horses. They gathered the three women and tied them with their hands at the small of their backs and lifted them in the back of the wagon. They pulled Hawkstone out from under the wagon, and kicked the Peacemaker from his hand, while four of them struck his torso with their fists. He hit two of them in the face, and when they grabbed his arms, he kicked a third.

A leader stood beside the ashes while the four held Hawkstone – big and burly, over six feet and 200 pounds, chisel face in the moonlight, and a cross-draw Colt .45 Peacemaker.

He stared at Hawkstone, his face unmoving stone. 'You don't cut the ranch fence.'

The mules were hitched and the mustangs tied behind. A ranch hand climbed up on the seat. With the tied women in the back of the wagon, he slapped the reins on the mules' backs and the wagon rolled away. Another ranch hand had lassoes around the necks of the buckskin and the grey. He led them off.

The leader stepped up to Hawkstone and hit him across the jaw. 'We're gonna bust you up, boy, and leave you in a hollow someplace. Teach you a lesson.'

'This is free range,' Hawkstone said. 'You don't fence free range.'

Another blow came across his other jaw. 'This is the Circle-X, drifter. We do any damn thing we want. Our land, our cattle. You let prime beef aimed for rich European and

51

British markets wander off. We got to round them up. You got to pay for that.'

Hawkstone writhed in their grip. He got his right arm loose and swung out at the leader, but missed. Two of the men holding him punched him hard in the back and side. Pain shot through him like pistol slugs.

The leader stood back. 'Who are you? What do you want here?'

'The name is Hawkstone. I came to sell mustangs.'

'They been confiscated, boy. Don't know what we'll do with the women. They your wives? You one of them Mormons?'

'No.'

'So, we'll put them to work.'

'No, you won't,' Hawkstone said. He stomped on the boot of a man on his right. The same two punched his back and side again.

'Hold him,' the leader said. 'Let's go to work on him.'

The blows hit hard and often, mostly around the ribs and head. Grunts of effort came from the men. Two held him while the other three punched their fists into him. As he started to lose sight and thought, he took the blows and stayed conscious enough to ask, 'Name?' At first they ignored him, just kept hitting. 'Name?' he mumbled again.

But then he could no longer think with reason. Blackness washed his thinking and his knees began to buckle.

The leader was speaking. 'Hook a lasso around his ankles and drag him to Splinter Hollow. Leave him there. If the wolves don't get him, the rattlers will. He won't have no food or water. He won't last long.'

'Be better off, we just shoot him,' another said.

'We ain't no killers, 'cept mebbe a few nesters rustling our cattle. No, let him bleed on out. If a miracle happens and he survives, so be it.' Saddle leather creaked as the leader mounted. 'See you boys back at the ranch.' Hooves pounded to fade as the horse galloped off.

A silence followed. Hawkstone tried to move but couldn't.

'Well, Willie, what you think?' one of the remaining two asked.

'I ain't draggin' no man behind no horse.'

'Me neither. We can drape him over my gelding and ride on out to Splinter Hollow. What's that he said?'

'Name. . . .' Hawkstone mumbled.

'What name you want, Hawkstone? Me, I'm Bowleg Bob. This here's Willie Wink. We ain't gonna drag you.'

They pulled him on to the neck of the gelding in front of the saddle horn. He stayed like that for more than an hour, twisting in pain with horse movements while the riders rode silent. When they got to where they were going, he was pushed off and fell on rocky ground surrounded by forest.

'Name?' he wheezed.

'What name? We told you ours. Willie, dig out your canteen. We ain't leavin' the man without water.'

A canteen was thrown down beside him. He fought to stay semi-conscious, but it was a losing battle. The ground was hard, rocky, dotted with tree limbs and logs.

The two horses turned to walk away. They stopped. They turned back.

'Willie, I think the jasper wants to know the name of the Bar-X foreman, the man who gives us orders.'

Bowleg Bob said, 'Hawkstone, his name be Ward Cameron. He's one mean *hombre*. But it ain't likely you'll be able to do anything with that.'

TEN

Morning sunlight came, but Hawkstone's eyes were punched too shut to see clearly. The light filtered as if through a wide waterfall. He blinked and turned his head. His body ached everywhere from the waist up. The area behind his left ear where the man, Ward Cameron, kicked him in the head hurt worst. The rest of him carried painful bruises, even a few ribs, though he didn't think any other bones were broken. This was no place he hadn't been before. But he wouldn't be forgetting Ward Cameron any time soon.

With effort, he reached for the canteen and paused to rest. More time and effort, and he gulped down two swallows of cool water. He laid back and opened his eyes enough so he was able to see trees around him. Pines grew about, and firs, with rough gnarled trunks, some thick as horses, their growth speared straight into drifting clouds, drooping branches trimmed in fanned green needles. The firs rose fifty feet or more with smaller trees between, standing a third as high and carrying uplifting, extended branches crowded in needles bunched along the branches, youth eager to grow fast and tall, looking like parlour Christmas trees waiting for decoration. Between the firs, aspen stood spindly with skinny grey branches that had broad leaves which fluttered in the breeze like attached bright emerald butterflies. The rocky ground he lay on carried a carpet of tan interwoven grass, spotted in brown pine cones and visible seedlings. Though not really in the mountains, this was high plain, almost too high for buffalo grass.

He tried to push up to sit, but his arms fought him in pain. The hour was too soon to think of hate. He knew the body healed itself. The bleeding had already stopped. His clothes were torn and bloody, but he would think of healing and fight back the pain. When he was healed enough to move around, there would be plenty of time for hate. And time for Ward Cameron. He was in a bad situation, sure enough. But it never occurred to him that he might die. He had water, thanks to Bowleg Bob and Willie Wink, and if he spared his swallows, it would last until he could move. Once he could stand, and even walk, all kinds of possibilities opened. But what made the situation worse were the overhead clouds that grew darker with each passing hour. He smelled moisture in the air. He had to crawl. He was on a slant angled down a shallow hill. Twenty feet from him the ground dropped into a ravine, which would fill with rushing water if the rain came heavy.

He fell asleep. Without being aware, he dropped off to unconsciousness, and falling raindrops woke him. How long was he out? Almost an hour. The cool rain gave him strength. He would crawl up, not down. Harder, but he didn't want to mud slide down to the ravine. With his fingers dug in the woven grass, he pulled his arms and pushed his knees, gritting against the pain. He went a foot, two feet. A cluster of three small pines hugged together with thick fresh branches of needles, sheltered by a tall old fir, like children clinging to their ma. He reached them and pushed between them, and the strength it took to get there sent him off to sleep again.

The shelter did not protect him completely. He woke, soaked and shivering to the hiss of rain over and through the high plain forest around him. He took a swallow from the canteen. Curled in the foetal position, he tried to force himself to stop shaking. He continued to shiver while the rain came down and hissed harder. He went to sleep again.

When next he woke, it was dark. The rain had lightened, yet the needles above him still dripped. His head jerked when he thought he heard a noise above him. He went back to sleep.

Raindrops plopped loud on a canvas sheet over his head. He lay next to a fallen log with the cover stretched across branches. It offered just enough room to sit under. A campfire out towards the edge where the rain didn't reach sent warmth that made him crawl closer. He was covered with a buffalo robe. A grey dawn showed a break in the clouds. Winks of sunlight flickered through. He wanted to holler a greeting, but that part of him didn't function yet. Boots came sliding down the hill above him and a big dark shadow ducked under the canvas to sit beside him.

'Thought I might have to bury you, old pard.'

Hawkstone lay quiet and stared at the man.

The man removed his dark grey slicker. Russet brown eyes, medium reddish-brown hair under a dirty, grey Montana Peak Stetson, no-collar medium grey flannel shirt buttoned to the throat, buckskin vest. He wore a Colt .45 low, leg-tied like a gunslinger. Firelight showed a bullet crease scar across the end of his nose. He had a three-day beard.

'Name is Brag Hailey,' he said. 'You're no lightweight, pard. Hefted you on my shoulder to get to this here log. Only place I could stretch the canvas. Somebody, or a few somebodies, punched you out good. That left eye will show some colour a week or more. We can talk when you feel able. Meanwhile, I got some antelope jerky, and this.' He held up a bottle of whiskey. 'Might be another day or so before

56

you're ready.'

He looked beyond the cover of the canvas to sunlight shadows. 'Under all them bruises, you must be around forty, same age as me. Ain't much good in life for us old timers no more. A reliable horse, an accurate gun, a good bottle of whiskey, a tender steak now and then, a poke with a soft, pliable, real pretty girl on occasion. Wish it were true, right old pard? You don't believe it no more than me. Usually what we get is some nag that trips over his own hoofs, a Peacemaker that misfires half the time, rotgut cut with kerosene, a tough hunk of shoe leather been worn across eight miles of prairie, and a fat, horse-face old pay-for-play who keeps telling you to hurry up, others are waiting.' He cocked his head and winked. 'Life ain't easy for us old timers no more, right, pard?'

Brag Hailey nursed his beaten charge along, helped him drink water, got a little food down him. The next day, the charge propped to his elbow.

'Brag Hailey,' he said. 'The name is Hawkstone, Anson Hawkstone. I'm obliged for your kindness.'

'You want to talk about the polecats worked you over?'

'Later, in a day or two. I feel my strength coming back.'

'How about a sip of the firewater?'

'I do believe I will.'

The next day, Hawkstone was sitting. He couldn't stand yet, but that would come. 'Brag,' he said. 'I got nothing. Except for my torn clothes, I'm naked in this world. They took everything.'

Brag Hailey grinned. 'Then we got to get it all back.'

'You got no part in this.'

'Unless I invite myself along.'

Hawkstone took down a slug of whiskey. It burned with the flow and let him know where many of the punches had

57

landed. He squinted at Hailey. 'Why?'

'I figure we're both men looking for something. Mebbe not the meaning of happiness – hell, that stage rolled out years ago – but you're here for something, and you got yourself in trouble getting too close. Me too. You want to tell me what it is?'

'I'm looking for a fella.'

Brag slapped his knee, 'Damned if I ain't too. I'm one of the last of the bounty hunters, though mebbe there always will be a place for us. The world is full of people running away – from the law, another man, a wife or woman. Another fella got to hunt them down. If they be killers meaner than jest regular criminals, they got to be put down.'

Hawkstone pulled the wrinkled wedding photo from his vest pocket. 'Ever seen this jasper around?'

'Well, I'll be a jackrabbit in a Saguaro cactus. I got a pitcher just like that, only not as pretty.' Brag unfolded a drawing of Linus Raines, a 'Wanted' poster with a reward of one thousand dollars. 'I aim to shoot the bastard dead as the ashes of love, and collect my reward.'

ELEVEN

By the third day Hawkstone could stand, though it was on the side of the slant. He looked up and saw there was a road above them. Brag Hailey kept his roan up there tethered to a fir. Hawkstone flexed and twisted, fighting back pain while he gained strength. He still needed too much sleep. At such times Brag left him alone and rode off.

On the third night, Brag plopped next to Hawkstone with a fresh bottle of whiskey and smoked ham. 'Been to Cheyenne a couple days,' he said. 'Heard tell of our boy. He was there, in the company of a Lindsey Kyle, cute daughter of Millie Kyle, who owns and runs the Circle-D out neighbourly to the Bar-X.'

Hawkstone took a slug of whiskey. 'Brag, I don't want you killing the boy.'

Brag cawed a short cough. 'For a thousand dollars, I got to ignore that request, old pard.'

'I got to take him home,' Hawkstone said. 'What if I said the sea captain I work for will see you get the thousand, plus a bonus?'

'Are you saying that?'

'I ain't got it, but he does. And he'll pay it.'

'Pay it, where?'

'San Francisco, when I get the boy back there.'

'Cry howdy, pard, that's a far piece to collect. I got the

polecat in my sights here and I can plug him at will. The thousand is here, waiting.'

Hawkstone handed the bottle to Brag. 'I'm asking.'

'Mebbe you ask too much, Hawkstone.'

'But I'm asking.'

'Does that mean I got to draw down on you if I decide to take him?'

Hawkstone put his elbows on his knees and stared at his boots. 'I don't want it to come to that.'

Brag rubbed his hand across his mouth. He handed the bottle back to Hawkstone. 'Well, we ain't caught up to the killer yet. Let me think on it. I didn't go to all the trouble saving your life jest to shoot you down like a rabid cur.' He pointed his gloved finger at Hawkstone. 'Don't think for one minute you can outdraw me, pard. I'm faster than one of them new-fangled light bulbs when you flick the switch. I come against some mean hombres, a lot of them thought they was faster. But they is dead and I'm still riding my old roan looking for more of them.'

'Think hard on it, Brag. I'm beholden to you, but I can't move away on this. I'm no gunfighter. Don't make us have a showdown.'

'Don't you, Anson Hawkstone,' Brag Hailey said.

The next day, after Hawkstone had made it to the road and back, and now rested under the canvas, he heard a rattling noise.

Brag came sliding down the slant. 'Pard, what you got to do with a wagon load of women?'

'Help me up to the road,' Hawkstone said.

Ruth Bowers was at the wagon reins, wearing her yellow dress. Nettie White and Yin Chun sat on the seat with her. A man rode alongside on a young bay. The man looked familiar.

Hawkstone stood on the road holding a fir for support

60

and grinned at them.

Ruth stared at him. 'God, Mr Hawkstone, you look awful.'

He nodded to the man on the bay. 'You look familiar, mister.'

He wore sheep-wool chaps and a Montana Peak hat, with a denim shirt and brown vest. His face was clean of whiskers and he had a very large nose. 'You ought to. I was one of them brought you here. Name is Willie Wink.'

'How many punches did I take from you?'

'Not me, sir. I just brought you here, me and Bowleg Bob. We didn't do no hitting. Cameron has plenty of hands for that. Me, I'm just a ranch hand. All I punch is cows, mebbe some ranch hands if I get too drunk.'

Nettie smiled at Willie. 'He helped us escape. They had us tied in a barn. We got Yin Chun loose and when the man came to feed us, she hit him over the head with a fireplace log. He didn't have no gun or we'd have brought it. Willie helped us get the wagon and mules. He showed us the way here. He's our hero.'

'He's *your* hero,' Ruth said.

Willie grinned at Nettie.

Ruth reached in the back of the wagon. 'I got your hat, Mr Hawkstone. Your pack is still back here so you can change clothes. But we couldn't find anything else, not your horses or the mustangs, or your gun. I got my single shot .410 you can use.' She pulled the wire cutters. 'You might need these.'

Hawkstone put on his hat and took the shotgun. 'Much obliged.' He looked up at Willie. 'Where is the man, Ward Cameron?'

Willie tore his gaze away from Nettie. 'There was a killing out to one of the nesters' farms. The head guy, in fact, Miles Trevor, up and found his son, Earl, shot dead. Folks think it's got something to do with the daughter, Janey-Jean, and an argument the boy had with somebody been fooling with her.

61

All she does is sit on the porch with her face in her hands and cry. Won't say nothing to nobody. Not even her pa.'

'Talk to me about Cameron.'

'He thinks the nesters rustled some prime beef set for Europe. Mebbe it was some of them got loose when you cut the fence. Anyway, he's out there to Trevor's place looking for them cows, and he don't give a cigarette stomp in the dirt about no nester's kid getting shot or some wisp of a girl bawling her eyes out.'

'He's out there now?' Hawkstone asked.

'Far as I know.'

Hawkstone looked over at Brag, who stood by the tied neck of his roan, watching and listening to every word. Hawkstone returned his gaze to Willie. 'I'd like the loan of your bay. You can ride with Nettie in the wagon. I'll bring it to you when I get my horses back.'

Will glanced at Nettie, then squinted at Hawkstone. 'Bring it, where?'

'You know the Circle-D ranch? Brag here was telling me about it.'

Willie nodded. 'Neighbour to the Bar-X.'

'Show Ruth the way.' He turned to Ruth. 'The woman who owns the place is Millie Kyle. Ask to stay with her until I get there.'

'Where are you going?' she asked.

'I'll be looking up this fellow, Ward Cameron.'

TWELVE

Linus Raines propped on a pillow next to Lindsey, her corn-silk hair on his chest. He reckoned Wyoming Territory was getting a little too hot for a Gypsy Man. At least the part down in the south-east section, between Cheyenne and Fort Laramie. He had seen the Wanted poster on the post office wall. Somebody was bound to come looking, especially for a thousand dollars. Maybe he ought to think about crossing over into Dakota Territory. Plenty of fellows were finding gold back in the Black Hills.

But he wasn't ready to give up the long-legged, slinky ranch owner's daughter.

Lindsey kissed his throat and said, 'What if Ma won't sell? What then, Linus? What if she won't listen to the bankers?'

'Where is she?' Linus asked.

'North. She hitched the buggy and went to the nester got his son shot. The man is so upset, he's talking about shooting some people himself. Four ranch hands went with her.' She snuggled closer. 'How we going to get the money to travel if my ma won't sell the ranch?'

Linus already had his mind working. 'What if something happened to Millie? I mean, God forbid, what if she had some kind of accident? The ranch would be yours, right?'

Lindsey lightly punched his caved-in hairless chest. 'Linus, you can't talk like that. Don't say things like that.

Nothing will happen to Ma. She's tough as a buffalo.'

'Ranch life can be dangerous.'

'How would you know? How many ranches you worked on?'

'Bones get broke. People fall, get kicked by a horse, have a tree fall on them.'

Lindsey pushed up. 'That won't happen to my ma. Listen. I hear horses. The buggy, or a wagon.'

Linus pushed out of bed and began to dress. He tried to see out the window but he was too far away and the shade was down. With his pants and shirt on, he crossed and peeked around the side of the shade to late afternoon sun. 'Millie and four riders. Got another wagon, looks like a prairie schooner of some kind, coming in from the other direction.' He let the shade fall. He sat on the bed and began pulling on his boots, careful to keep the bowie inside the boot in its sheath. 'I know the driver. He's a ranch hand from the Bar-X, goes by Willie Wink.'

'What do they want?' Lindsey said. She was already in her dress and brushing her hair.

When Linus stepped on to the front porch, he couldn't believe his eyes.

Millie halted the one-horse buggy next to the porch. 'Take the reins, Linus. What were you doing in the house?'

'Killing a spider for Lindsey.' But Linus didn't take the reins. He stood on the porch and stared at the wagon with the two mules.

'I told you to take the reins,' Millie said. Millie looked tired. Her grey hair was piled up and the wrinkles of sixty-some years were etched deep in her face with tiredness. Wispy strands of her grey hair spider-webbed around her ears and neck. Her tan plains hat was tilted back. 'What the hell you looking at, boy?'

One of the ranch hands swung down from his mount and took the reins and tied the buggy off to the porch hitching rail.

64

'Christ on a bronc,' Linus said watching the wagon.

Lindsey came on to the porch, fluffing her shoulder-length corn-silk hair.

'Aiee!' Yin Chun cried. She climbed over Willie and Nettie and jumped down to the wagon wheel and almost fell to her knees when she landed on the ground. With little pause, she ran straight for Linus and started pounding on his chest. 'You, bad Gypsy Man. You get me like this. I kill you, lizard face. I kill you!'

'What the hell are you doing here?' Linus screeched as he backpedalled. He bumped into the house wall and could go no farther. A flash of thought had the bowie in his hand, but he thought again. He did the first act that came to mind. He drew his Remington, ready to blow her chink, slant-eye head clean off her shoulders.

But Millie had her two-barrel twelve-gauge aimed straight for his belly. 'Drop it to the porch, boy. I'll cut you in half if you don't.'

Yin Chun stood back, heaving, her belly protruding. Linus almost swung to aim the Remington toward Millie. One of the ranch hands had his Peacemaker in hand, aimed for Linus' head. Even Willie Wink had a revolver aimed at him. Linus dropped the Remington and slipped two steps along the wall. He would have to find an opening to reach for his boot.

Yin Chun slapped his face then back-handed him. She looked at Millie. 'Shoot him!'

Linus had his arms crossed in front of his face. He only had one thought – flight. The Dakota Hills looked mighty attractive right then.

Milly turned to her ranch hands. 'Somebody get his hands tied behind him.'

Linus turned to Lindsey, who stared at him like he was cockroach just crawling up the porch steps. 'Lindsey, I can explain all this. It's a big mistake.'

65

Yin Chun leaped at him again. She hit his ear and nose and neck. He pushed her shoulder, then grabbed her across the breasts and pulled her in front of him. He jerked her back against him. He felt a pistol push on his temple.

'Drop your arms to your sides,' the ranch hand said.

'I got a rope,' Willie Wink called as he dropped from the wagon seat and stepped to the porch. He made quick, tight work of Linus' hands behind his back. He picked up the Remington and stuck it in his belt.

'You give me gun,' Yin Chun said.

'No, ma'am,' Willie said. He squinted at Linus. 'How come you look familiar?'

Millie had put her shotgun down. 'What are you saying?' She frowned at Willie, then at Lindsey, then the wagon. 'Who are you people? What do you want here?'

Willie said, 'I think there's a "Wanted" poster on this here fella. I seen it in Cheyenne.'

'Mistaken identity,' Linus said. He turned to Lindsey.

She shrank away from him. 'Don't come near me.'

Millie turned to her ranch hands. 'Take him to the barn. Tie him to one of the posts. I'll send somebody for the sheriff. We'll see what's what about this.' She looked at Yin Chun's belly. 'I don't know what can be done about you. He done did his business.'

'The baby not connected to him no more,' Yin Chun said. 'It is my baby. We go to Oregon and find my family and I beg them to forgive me. We open restaurant in Oregon.'

Linus said, 'Yin Chun.'

'You shut face. You go to jail now. Good place for you.'

Millie climbed off the buggy and again looked at Ruth and Nettie on the wagon seat. 'I asked, who the hell are you people?'

Ruth said, 'You must be Millie. If I can step down from here I'll explain everything to you.' When Millie nodded, Ruth pushed off the wagon seat. 'There is a man, Anson

66

Hawkstone, who wants to sell you a few broken mustangs. We're sort of with him, so we came here to wait.'

Two ranch hands began to march Linus off the porch.

Millie said, 'I'm always in the market for horses. Why do you have to wait?'

'He has to get them back from the men who stole them,' Ruth said.

THIRTEEN

The sun hid behind the Rockies when Brag and Hawkstone rode on to Bar-X property. The fence had been repaired with a double strand across the break, but Hawkstone carried his wire cutters from the wagon and cut it in a different section. He and Brag rode through and walked their ponies for the buildings.

Brag said, 'That will upset some folks.'

Hawkstone turned to him. 'You think open prairie needs fencing?'

'Nope. But you and me ain't more'n coffee grounds in a tin cup when it comes to big decisions about open range. Ranch owners got the say, not fellas like us.'

Hawkstone said, '*He that is rich need not live sparingly, and he that can live sparingly need not be rich.*'

Brag stared at him. 'Where in a blustery wind did that come from?'

'It's a Ben Franklyn. Now and then I spout a few words to suit the occasion.'

'Don't you believe the rich rule the world?'

'Only what they can get their hands on. Do they rule your world?'

'Not so's anybody would notice. But I ain't got much. I can push along on my own jest fine. They sure rule all around it, though.'

68

Hawkstone nodded. 'If I can carry a pair of wire cutters, nobody will fence off my path across the range.'

'Ward Cameron didn't teach you a lesson about that?'

'Cameron is about to learn his own painful lesson,' Hawkstone said.

They rode straight for the big ranch house. Brag peeled off and waited outside the shack where cowhands bunked.

'Ward Cameron!' Hawkstone called. He dismounted and tied the bay to the hitch rail in front of the water trough. He pulled Ruth's shotgun and held it easy.

A woman came on the porch. She had spectacles low on her nose and frowned at him with curiosity. She wore buckskin pants and a blue flannel shirt to compliment cool, muted, medium-blue cornflower eyes. She looked about twenty-five, tiny and frail with small shoulders.

'He's not here,' she said in a high, squeaky voice. She looked hard at his battered face and squinted.

Behind Hawkstone, the bunkhouse door opened and three gun-holstered ranch hands came out. Brag sat on his roan with his Colt in his hand. He nodded to the horse trough in front of the three. 'Drop the gun belts in the trough, boys, and rest easy.'

The boys did as they were told. They sat on a bench in front of the building.

The woman removed her spectacles and frowned. 'Who are you?' Her voice was screechy as a badly played violin. 'What happened to you?'

'Name is Hawkstone, ma'am, here to get stolen property of mine and deal with a hard case goes by the name of Ward Cameron. And you are?'

'Caroline Shelby. I own this ranch. I don't know anything about any stolen property.'

'No, ma'am. Where is Cameron?'

She stood with a fist holding the spectacles on her right hip. 'I don't think I'm going to tell you.'

69

'Yes'm, you are, or I'll cut the rest of your illegal fences and let all them expensive cows run around loose for the taking.'

Her hand went to her throat. 'You cut my fence?'

'Yes'm.' Hawkstone stepped to the porch. 'You got six mustang mares of mine. Where?' He stepped to her and towered over her, causing her to shrink from his height. 'You got my buckskin mare and rig, and my old grey pack horse. And Cameron took my Colt Peacemaker when he and his gang jumped me.'

'He said you let prime beef get out.'

'And that's just the beginning if I don't get my property back, right now. Where is he?'

'Among the sodbusters, looking for our cows. I understand the Trevor boy got himself killed, something over the girl, Janey-Jean and a boy, Linus Raines.'

Hawkstone stepped back and frowned. 'What was that name again? Raines?'

The woman blinked at him. 'That's what I heard. Miles Trevor is on a killing rampage looking for him. We think the nesters rustled some of our beef. That's why Ward is there.'

'And my property?'

'I told you, I don't know anything about your property.'

'Yes'm, and you're lying.'

'Hawkstone!' Brag called. 'A corral out behind the barn.'

Hawkstone shoved the shotgun into the back of his belt. With his hands on her slender shoulders, he gently pulled Caroline Shelby around to the side. He took one step and tried the ranch-house door. She had locked it when she came to the porch. Standing back, he pulled the shotgun free and kicked at the lock enough to splinter most of it. A second kick sent the door cracking open.

'What are you doing?' she cried.

'Does Cameron stay in the house?'

'I'm not that kind of woman, mister.'

70

Hawkstone went in and marched towards carpeted stairs. 'We already know you're a liar. No telling what else you are.' On the way to the stairs, he saw a den with desk and chairs and walls lined with books. He went in. He whiffed a bookish trace, but mostly smelled man-sweat odour. The sweat of effort, the kind of effort a man might use beating on another man. Nothing sure. A lot of sweat poured while those boys punched him in the night. But a man had been in the den.

Hawkstone opened desk drawers and rifled through them and tossed the paper contents left and right to the floor. A lower right-side door was locked. He swung the shotgun around and blasted the drawer lock. The crack of the shot echoed through the house. When he slid it open he saw two revolvers. One was his Colt .45 Peacemaker. It slipped easy into his empty holster. The other was an old Remington. He checked to find it loaded, shoved it in the back of his belt, and picked up the empty shotgun.

Now for his horses.

Caroline Shelby stood outside the den door. She looked on the verge of tears. Hawkstone shoved past her and headed back outside.

'He'll kill you for this,' she said. 'I know him. He won't sit still for an invasion of our privacy. He'll shoot you down.'

'I hope he tries,' Hawkstone said.

Outside in front of the bunkhouse, Brag had the three ranch hands bound against the hitch rail and was sitting on his roan waiting. They rode around the barn to the corral where the mustangs pranced. The buckskin and the grey were with them.

Inside the barn, Hawkstone found his Mexican saddle and bridle. He eased his buckskin away from the others and saddled her. He and Brag quietly moved the mustangs and grey, and Willie Wink's bay out of the corral and towards the east.

71

'Where to?' Brag asked.

'The neighbour ranch. What's it called? The Circle-D. The wagon ought to be there waiting.'

'There'll be another wire fence.'

Hawkstone clicked to the mustangs while he lightly twirled his lasso. 'We'll deal with it. I hear our boy has been fooling with one of the nester girls, hear tell he even shot down her brother. The nesters are in a fit looking for him. Cameron is there.'

'Mebbe I should jest go on out there and wait.'

'Raines wouldn't be there, not after a killing.' They moved with the horses across the range with patches of rich green grass, broken by hoof-stomped dirt. The mustang mares tossed their heads and ran loose. Hawkstone also had Willie Wink's bay in tow. 'I never figured the boy as a killer.'

'The poster is for a girl's daddy. No telling how many others.'

'We'll find him.'

'And I'll shoot him down,' Brag Hailey said.

FOURTEEN

Millie Kyle walked around the corral studying the mustangs. The morning sun pierced a clear sky and washed the prairie and mountains in brightness. She shielded her eyes with the flat of her hand to help her hat brim shade her. She had golden amber eyes set in a creased face.

'Mr Hawkstone, you show some trouble.'

'Yes'm. Ward Cameron still has his coming.'

'Keep it off my ranch.' She nodded to the mustangs. 'They good to ride?'

'I've ridden them around campsites.'

'How much do you want?'

'Eighty each.'

She shook her head. 'They're young. I'll give you sixty if you stay long enough to work cattle with them.'

Hawkstone lifted his boot to the corral rail. 'That would take mebbe a month or more. And they'd be worth a hundred. If your ranch hands know their horses they can work cattle with them in a couple weeks. Make it seventy.'

'Seventy it is then. That include the grey? That grey ain't worth no seventy.'

'No, the grey is my pack horse.'

Millie stood directly in front of Hawkstone. 'What about them women? They belong to you?'

'No, ma'am. They'd be looking for temporary work.'

'Got some laundry and cleaning and cooking they might do for found and keep. I got a deputy sheriff on his way out from Cheyenne, on account of the boy tied in the barn. Should be here about noon.'

'I heard about him. Think I'll go have a looksee. I may take the boy with me before the deputy gets here.'

Millie looked towards the ranch house where Brag Hailey and Willie Wink walked towards them, Brag with his slight leg-wound limp. She frowned at Hawkstone, which deepened the wrinkles in her face. She pulled the brim of her plains hat lower. 'You figure to buck the law, Mr Hawkstone?'

'Yes'm. Linus Raines does me no good shut away in a jail cell.'

Millie nodded to Brag. 'I seen the wanted poster. You a bounty hunter?'

Hawkstone pointed at Brag. 'He is. I got personal business with the boy.'

'What about that Oriental blossom in a family way?'

'Yin Chun has made her peace with the situation. The women will soon be on their way to Oregon. I'll be taking them to the Trail. Could be the ranch hand, Willie Wink, is riding along.'

'He hankers after the Sioux captive,' Millie said, 'Nettie White.'

'White Leaf. Yes'm, I believe he does.'

Millie studied Hawkstone. 'You're a rough one all right. My little girl is flighty and irresponsible. She ain't dumb, but she don't apply herself, especially with men. She's lazy and her daddy spoiled her. I want a man for Lindsey, a real man. I talked to her about that sleazy juvenile boy, and about how a man like you might sweep her off her feet.'

Hawkstone watched the two men come from the house. 'I got a woman and she's all I want to handle.' He let the words fall out there to the ground where they lay without need for further comment.

74

Millie nodded, and waited until the other two men reached them. She looked from one to the other. 'I may need all your guns, gentlemen. I got seven riders. The Coslet brothers told me they spotted Bar-X beef on nester land when they were fence riding. Then there's the girl whose brother got shot down by our guest in the barn. Willie tells me the Bar-X foreman is a hothead who jumps before he thinks.'

Hawkstone turned to Willie. 'He's right. I told you, his name is Ward Cameron.'

'I knew that,' Millie said. 'He brags he's going to burn the nesters out. Cut every wire they strung and strip them to ashes. I don't care as long as they don't touch my place. But somehow, I don't see that happening. If I don't stop them, this whole valley will go up in flames.'

Brag looked at Hawkstone, then turned to Millie. 'What about the sheriff? Cheyenne seems to have plenty of deputies, what with deputy marshals and vigilantes. Get them to do something.'

The mustangs pranced inside the corral. In unison, they looked off to the north. Hawkstone saw smoke on the horizon, a thin line barely visible.

Millie said, 'Deputies are only interested in Cheyenne problems. They're so hell-bent to make this territory a state they got blinders on to what else is happening. The boom of Texas cattle being driven up here is over. Prices are dropping. There are just too many coming. We got sections of open range far as the eye can see where not a blade of grass is growing. We got to fence them out. We here at the Circle-D specialize to a European market and the wire keeps our beef from being cross-bred and the grass from disappearing.'

Hawkstone turned away. 'What do you want, sympathy?'

Millie stood tall. 'I want your guns, in case the hothead foreman decides to spread his influence beyond nesters and their pathetic farms.'

Hawkstone pointed to the line of smoke to the north. 'Looks like he's started.'

Millie turned towards the ranch house. 'If there's gunplay, I want it out there, not here on my place. I'll get your payment, I assume you want gold coin.'

'Yes'm,' Hawkstone said.

'Will you ride out with my boys and see what's going on?'

Hawkstone looked towards the barn. 'Soon as I chew some words with the boy in there.'

Brag stepped up beside Hawkstone. 'I reckon I'll poke along beside you, old pard.'

As soon as they entered the barn, Brag unsnapped the rawhide loop over his Colt hammer. The bullet crease across the tip of his nose shined like a piece of fishing line. 'Don't stop me, Hawkstone.'

Hawkstone had to figure a way to keep the boy alive. He had a coming deputy to deal with, and now Brag was ready to gun Raines down.

'Not here, not now,' Hawkstone said.

'What's to stop me?'

'I'm asking you, Brag. Trouble is starting through this valley. Let's help deal with it first. Then we can come back to the cockroach.'

They looked around the barn. Across, at one of the support poles, Hawkstone saw cut ropes and a plate of food. Brag went past it to a hay pile and started pushing his boot through it. He uncovered the body of Al Coslet, one of the Coslet brothers.

Brag let out a curse. 'The bastard had a knife. He cut Al's throat.'

Raines was gone.

FIFTEEN

Linus Raines galloped his sorrel hard. He rode out of the valley, bypassed Cheyenne, only to learn outside a roadside saloon that the 'Wanted' poster was now up to two thousand dollars, dead or alive. He carried his canteen but had no food, and only the twelve silver dollars Al Coslet had in his jeans pocket. He had to get out of Wyoming Territory, into Dakota Territory and grab some gold in the Black Hills, either from the ground or a miner's pockets.

For weapons he had his trusty eight-inch bowie knife and Al Coslet's Remington pistol. He had no spare ammunition.

When he reached the Dakota Territory border, the sun had dipped behind the Rockies. He did not intend to run his horse to ground. He had rested the sorrel on occasion. Now he slowed to a walk. There was plenty of grass to feed on and many creeks flowed towards the Platte river. In a day or two he would bypass Wounded Knee and enter the Black Hills.

Always aware of possible pursuit, he needed somebody to feed on, like a dumb farm girl. There were plenty of them around if he found one young enough. Ever since Martha, his cute wife out in San Francisco, he had been honing his skills, ever alert to avoid those too smart who might see right through his nonsense. He now knew what girls wanted to hear and he had no hesitation to say the words. If they wanted to talk love and marriage, he would happily oblige. He would tell them whatever was necessary, offer the lie of future and stability to get what he wanted, be it food, money or affection.

And he was hungry for all three.

Forty miles out of Fort Meade in Dakota Territory, Wade Beryl had a medium-size claim that he worked with a long tom and rocker and copper pan. A one-man operation, the claim sided a creek along an isolated draw between ragged hills. Wade had built a three-room cabin, and he pulled out enough gold for his own and his daughter's needs, plus a little extra he saved in a coffee pouch that he wanted to apply to the lumber business back in Springfield, Illinois, which was now being run by his wife and brother.

When Linus Raines heard this from seventeen-year-old Annie-Mae Beryl, he didn't give a whit about any lumber business in Illinois. The brother was probably fooling with the wife anyway, just as Linus had been fooling with Annie-Mae, a little too plump for his personal taste but certainly a girl with the right attitude. She appeared to believe everything he told her. What Linus wanted was that coffee pouch and everything else in the cabin he could carry away with him, especially silverware and the Winchester and shotgun, and the Colt .45 Peacemaker in the slick new-bought holster, and the Texas and Mexican saddles. He'd pack everything he needed on one of the two strong mules, and if he had to, he'd take Annie-Mae as far as needed away from Daddy, or Daddy's body, and drop her off somewhere on the trail along the way. And when he thought of Texas, he thought it might be a good place to settle, down around El Paso or farther, Laredo, maybe even dip across the border for young senoritas, not too old or too bright, and where no 'Wanted' posters would reach.

For now, though, after four days out of Wyoming

Territory, he had just met Annie-Mae, and camped less than a mile from the claim. She came to him and brought him food, and was impressed enough she wanted him to meet her daddy. They only had short lengths of time together because she had to help Daddy work the claim, since there was only the two of them. The nearest civilization was the mining camp three miles away.

On the fourth night, Annie-Mae said she might love Linus. He told her he loved every inch of her fully developed woman body, and he was ready to meet Daddy. He told her it was only fitting after he met Daddy that he should help work their claim.

At his one-canvas-sheet camp, Linus Raines made sure the old Remington functioned well, then he saddled the sorrel and swung into the saddle. He had no idea what Annie-Mae had been telling Daddy about the new boy she met who was about to stake a claim less than a mile away, and wanted to learn prospecting by helping. He would handle this meeting with Daddy as it played.

Annie-Mae rode her magnificent palomino stallion halfway to meet him. She dressed in a split-skirt brown velvet riding dress that draped over the saddle like a tent. The palomino would be something else Linus intended to take with him. Might be worth more than two hundred dollars to an admirer of horseflesh looking to breed. Annie-Mae's chubby chipmunk face showed all grin when she saw him, and she leaned across to give him a wet kiss and waited while he caressed the soft parts of her he admired most.

'Daddy is anxious to meet you, honey-bunny.'

He kissed her again. She liked the pet name that made his teeth hurt each time he heard it, but he put up with it. 'Did you fix something to eat?'

'Fried chicken and dumplings, and carrots from our garden.'

'Good girl.' One thing Linus had to admit, Annie-Mae was a decent cook. And he was hungry.

They rode beside each other towards the claim. He fixed his face in a smile and forced himself to look at her the entire way. He decided what she had was baby fat. Not blubbery flesh that waddled when she moved, as it would while she grew older, but firm-skin puffy arms and legs and chubby cheeks, and a protruding soft belly. Her hair carried the colour of wild coyote strands, and was about as soft stringing to the back of her neck. She splashed herself with lilac water, and a lot of it. As they approached the cabin in darkness, windows lit with kerosene lanterns, Linus found himself thinking fondly of slender, long-legged Lindsey Kyle. He wanted to see her again, wanted to hold her. He also thought of the eager nester farm girl, Janey-Jean Trevor, and her buck-tooth smile, but she wasn't about to inherit a big ranch with thousands of cattle.

Wade Beryl stared and studied as he gripped the hand of Linus. In cabin lantern light, he was a mountain of a man, hump-shouldered with a thick mop of grey hair that blended with a beard and hid his chin, neck, and the top half of the bib overalls over his chest. His big hands were calloused and creek wrinkled. He was suspicious, and it showed in the slits of his dark eyes. They sat to eat and Wade spoke a blessing to the Lord, while Linus pretended to drop his gaze and glanced around the kitchen, eating table, parlour room, looking for a hiding place the man might keep gold. Annie-Mae babbled with her mouth full, mostly about Linus and how he wanted to learn how to get gold out of the creek and ground, and how he was about to file his own claim, and how he'd sure be obliged if Wade would show him how to do all that. Wade Beryl grunted his response while he concentrated on fried chicken and dumplings and carrots from their garden.

Suspicion did not leave the table. Before supper was over,

Linus knew he would not win Daddy over. Wade knew what Linus wanted from his daughter and from the cabin. Linus knew he could not take Annie-Mae away from Daddy, it would have to be Daddy's body. And maybe she would have to stay in the cabin with Daddy.

When the chicken was gone and the three of them sipped lemonade, Wade remained silent while Annie-Mae stood and cleared the table. Linus felt the pressure of hostility in the air. It was the same as when Earl caught him with Janey-Jean and had that ancient relic revolver aimed at him while his hand was up her dress.

It looked like the end here would have to be the same.

Wade Beryl pulled a briar pipe and began stuffing tobacco in the bowl. Annie-Mae was at the sink pumping water. Linus felt his chest flutter. His right hand shook. He stared at his lemonade glass.

'What's the matter with you, boy?' Wade said.

Linus said nothing. He licked his lips. His hand was under the table at his belly, a grip on the Remington.

Wade lit the pipe. 'I don't know you, boy, but I know your type. You look slick as a weasel.' He blew smoke. 'I don't believe one word of your fairy tale, you are filing a claim, you want to hook up with my Annie-Mae in a permanent way, help me work my stake. You're here to steal, boy, and mebbe worse. I want you outta my house and away from my little girl.'

He said no more.

Annie-Mae spun around with her plump face creased in a frown. 'Daddy! Don't say those things.'

Linus pulled the Remington and shot Wade through the left eye. The cabin roared with the blast. He cocked and his next shot shattered pipe and teeth. Gun smoke puffed around inside the table. Linus jerked the chair back and jumped to his feet as Wade broke the back of his chair going down to the floor. Linus shot the big man again in the chest.

Annie-Mae dropped a plate. It shattered to the floor almost as loud as the gunshots. 'Honey-bunny, what did you do?'

Her mouth opened wide in fear and horror as Linus swung the Remington around towards her, cocked the hammer and fired again. For an instant she stood, frowning. She leaned back against the counter as a dot of blood appeared on her forehead. When the trickle of blood eased over her nose and lips, her knees buckled and she fell forwards, causing the pine floor to vibrate with the sudden weight.

His heart slamming like a rockslide against his chest, the first thought Linus had was to make sure. He stepped over to where Annie-Mae lay and fired twice through the back of her head. He pulled the trigger again but the Remington clicked empty. No matter. There were plenty of guns and ammunition in the cabin. And gold. He knew there was hidden gold and he'd find it.

Then what would he do?

He had already decided. He wanted Lindsey Kyle and that ranch. Not the ranch, but the kind of money selling it would bring. He was going back, but just to pass through, collecting as he went.

Enjoy the girl, and take her money.

SIXTEEN

It had taken a week for Hawkstone to work the mares with cowhands so they moved cattle well. He grumbled to himself while doing so, though it was his own idea to help the woman out. The young outlaw Raines was getting away. Wade Cameron and the boys from the Bar-X had all but destroyed nester property. Half their farms were burned out. The nester men had taken their women and children by wagons farther north and set up camps within foothill valleys. Men gathered to grumble about the law and rights, to shout and point fingers in the air as they vowed revenge against the Bar-X. They collected all the weapons they had, preparing for a showdown.

This was reported to Millie and Hawkstone by the Circle-D appointed scout, Joe Coslet, who let it be known he wanted no part of scouting. He wanted to take off after the polecat Linus Raines who had slit his brother's throat, go after him like that bounty hunter, Brag Hailey.

Circle-D ranch hands rounded up most of the five thousand head and kept them closer to the ranch. The cattle were noisy and before long had eaten most of the close-by grass, then began to wander off looking for more. Creeks could barely provide the ten gallons a day each steer required. The cattle needed all the hundreds of thousands of acres the ranch provided. Wire fence gates were opened to provide them access to more open range, and they encroached on to Bar-X land.

In addition to what was going on, bankers came out from Cheyenne every other day in their stiff-looking suits driving a fancy buggy, and the price offer kept rising. Millie told Hawkstone she was about to throw up her hands and let the banks have it all. Lindsey encouraged her so they might live a good life in downtown Denver, or go back east to Chicago or New York City where civilized people lived. Lindsey was the result of east coast girl school ideas even though she'd been kicked out of three. She had enjoyed the style of living, it was the restriction and learning she didn't care for.

After three or four days, Joe Coslet reported directly to Hawkstone. He looked a lot like his deceased brother, Al, same hat, a bright green kerchief, except Joe, at twenty, sported a handsome black handlebar mustache. Joe and Hawkstone had the same goal: find the young outlaw – only, like the bounty hunter Brag Hailey, Joe wanted the killer dead. Joe said Ward Cameron and his gang kept finding Bar-X cattle on the nester land, so they burned down more farms. Every wire fence they came to they cut down. The whole north end of the valley had become a blanket of flames.

When Miles Trevor, the leader of the nesters, had been shot down in the dark, sporadic gunfire had started, and three of Cameron's Bar-X men were killed. Trevor hung on to life for two days, surrounded by his wife and daughters. His death was a signal for the final showdown.

The mustangs were ridden daily by ranch hands to help work ornery steers. Cowboys knew horses and beef. What they didn't like was forty to fifty nesters armed and mad and looking for a fight. Most cowhands had drifted through enough ranches for work and they knew the nesters wouldn't stop at the Bar-X. In the bunkhouse, they told Hawkstone the fight was coming to the Circle-D, and they didn't hire on at thirty a month and found to throw lead. The more peaceable cowboys among them thought maybe the nesters might be talked to, reasoned with – somebody might act as spokesman, and they all looked at Hawkstone, who met them with a cold stare of silence.

He pointed out that if any one of them had everything they worked for and owned taken away, crops destroyed, animals run off, buildings burned to the ground, their leader killed, how reasonable would they be? Nothing followed but silence. Hawkstone added that he wasn't getting thirty a month and found. He was passing through, after a killer outlaw he had to take back to San Francisco. And he had to get on with it before the jasper got himself killed. All the rest of what was going on just happened, and was basically none of his business.

With ten ranch hands on the Bar-X and seven with the Circle-D, they were no match against forty to fifty angry armed nesters. Hawkstone was concerned about his wagon women. He wanted them away from the ranch and trouble. They were eager to get on the Oregon Trail. The end of May was coming, the perfect time to leave. If they waited too many weeks longer they'd hit the high Rockies passes during blizzards and freezing cold. They had their token man, Willie Wink, who, because of his affection for Nettie White, intended to go with them and settle somewhere in Oregon Territory, likely out in the Willamette Valley, with Nettie as his wife. He drew no opposition from her.

The women wanted Hawkstone to lead them all, him being older and more trail experienced, but they knew he would be hard to convince. They told him they knew he wanted to get the worthless outlaw back to San Francisco, alive if possible, then return to his special woman waiting there in that Apache village down in the Arizona Territory. If he could just go with them part way, he might show Willie some twists and turns of the trail.

Ward Cameron and his ranch hands still conducted raids on nester property. He no longer confiscated just Bar-X beef, he helped himself to any other wandering cows, be they from nesters or the Circle-D. He and his gang picked off a nester whenever they had a chance. With two more Bar-X gang killed, they were down to eight.

It was a Saturday morning when Hawkstone and Joe hiked from the bunkhouse to the main ranch building. Joe had just returned from the east end of the valley.

'Cameron is going about it roundabout,' Joe said.

'Over what?'

'He's having his gang talk to our boys, putting out feelers. He ain't about to talk to you direct. He knows you're eventually coming for him on account of the beating he and the boys did to you.'

'He's right there,' Hawkstone said.

'He needs help. He figures all of us together might give the nesters a decent fight.'

'Why would Millie give a damn about the Bar-X?'

Joe glanced sideways at Hawkstone and twitched his thick mustache. ' 'Cause once they ride over the Bar-X, where you think they're headed next? We can't hold off that bunch.'

Willie Wink came out of the ranch house with a cup of coffee. He carried the air of a woman-satisfied man, a man in love and happy about it. He stopped and sipped as Joe and Hawkstone approached.

'Mornin', gents,' Willie said.

Hawkstone said, 'You know what's coming, Willie.'

'I do.'

'The women can't be here.'

'Where then, Fort Laramie?'

'You know where I healed up after the beating, Splinter Hollow? The road above where I was? You guided the wagon there.'

'I know it.'

'Take the wagon and the women and camp for a couple days. Then swing by here on your way to Fort Laramie.'

Willie sipped his coffee. 'What about Millie and Lindsey?'

Hawkstone pulled makings from his vest pocket. 'You won't get Millie out of here if you hog tie her. Try to convince Lindsey.'

'Why don't you convince her? She's looking at you with interest.'

'Which is why I'm out of it. Mebbe it's the women ought to talk to her. Millie, too.'

Willie said, 'I'll toss the words out, see where they land, watch the reception. You know, Millie wants us to meet the guns out there on the range, not here at the ranch.'

Hawkstone put the rolled cigarette between his lips and struck the match on the back of his Levi's leg. He lit and inhaled the smoke and blew it straight out. He offered the pouch but it was declined. 'It's wide open out there, no place for cover. I figure we hit and run. Cut a few down and ride for another cover. If we stay mounted and spread we might make a good accounting before we got to high-tail and run.'

Joe sighed deep. 'They'll cut through this place the way a scythe swipes through raw wheat. Won't be nothing here but ashes.'

Willie said, 'Except what I heard from Nettie, what Lindsey told her about Cheyenne.'

Hawkstone and Joe stared at Willie. 'About what?' Hawkstone said.

Willie sipped his coffee. 'You know Caroline Shelby, over to the Bar-X?'

'She owns it,' Joe said.

'She was in Cheyenne. She hired herself twenty gunslinger deputy vigilantes at fifty dollars a head to come out and help take care of the nesters.'

'When?' Hawkstone said.

'On their way now.'

The nesters spent all night Saturday cutting fences around both ranches. Cattle began to drift over open range headed through southern and central Wyoming Territory.

Sunday morning forty-three guns hit the Bar-X ranch with full force.

SEVENTEEN

With all fences cut there was no obstacle to riders crossing the range. The vigilantes rode hard directly for the Bar-X, twenty of them, their horses pounding the grass with open range fury, each rider likely already having killed men in towns or along trails in their past.

Hawkstone remembered the vigilantes in San Francisco as a young lad before he shipped out to sea. City government there was more corrupt than most, though he considered all governments corrupt. From the mayor to the council to the town marshal and his deputies, everybody was in bed with everybody else. Palms were greased and high dollars changed hands daily. When they'd had enough, shop keepers and store owners and stagecoach operators, and café and restaurant men, and a few professional gunmen, organized into a vigilante group. The gunmen made quick work of marshals and deputies, and the group openly swept through the City Council and all government offices and marched the men down to the Barbary Coast and hung them all. They then declared an election for a new government, and disbanded.

A year later, when that government got out of hand with corruption, the vigilantes got together and struck again with another mass hanging. They then again disbanded. The deputy vigilantes of Cheyenne were not of the same calibre.

These were hired thugs, quick-draw killers doing what the masters who paid them dictated. And now twenty of them worked for Caroline Shelby.

Joe Coslet led the Circle-D riders away from the ranch to the middle of the range between the two ranches. Hawkstone rode outside the group, the buckskin running hard. Yes, he knew of vigilantes, and his concern was for after. From what he remembered of his meeting with Caroline Shelby, she would not be riding anywhere. She had the money, but she did not have the force. She would turn over command of the vigilantes to her foreman, Ward Cameron. Under his orders, the vigilantes would shoot down every nester on a horse, save what they could of the Bar-X, maybe the main ranch house, then they would go after the nester wagons in the foothills and burn them out.

Then what? How ambitious was Cameron? Would the gang ride out to the Circle-D where only Millie waited? Willie had said several times that Ward Cameron made no secret to ranch hands of his lust for Lindsey. Cameron even hinted that with Caroline as his mistress, he might take Lindsey as his wife and control both ranches. No end to his confidence and conceit. Burned buildings could always be rebuilt, constructed the way a man in charge wanted.

Hawkstone intended to make sure Cameron never reached the Circle-D.

The nesters hit the Bar-X an hour before the vigilantes got there. Outbuildings were torched first. Any ranch hand that rode into view was cut down. Windows were shot out, torches thrown in the bunkhouse, and finally the ranch house itself.

Joe Coslet came on to the ranch firing his Winchester. He dropped two right away. Hawkstone had his Peacemaker drawn. A slug chipped the horn of his saddle. He spotted the shooter and cut him off his horse with a shot to the chest. They were a ragged bunch. Several sat bareback, others had no boots or shoes. Their weapons were old and inaccurate. Hawkstone wasn't sure that just the hands from both ranches couldn't take them.

Dirt and grass kicked by horses exploded along the near horizon as the gang of vigilantes swept on to the ranch at mid-day, some dressed as gamblers, some as cowhands, some as farmers, guns in hand, firing at any man in sight, aiming mostly at poor-looking riders with old weapons.

The nesters never had a chance.

Gunshots pulsed the air around the ranch. Men took cover where they could. Many stayed on their mounts riding between shacks and buildings. Smoke got caught in a wind and blew over spotty green range grass. Heat and sparks from buildings jumped to others. Men cried and shouted. Many were shot as they reloaded their old pistols.

Hawkstone looked for Cameron. He saw Caroline stagger from the burning ranch house, her blouse and face stained with soot. She held a small case as she stumbled on to the porch, looking tiny and frail. Daylight became blotted by flame and smoke. The barn and stables were mostly gone. She leaned against a porch wall, her waist-length blonde hair looking straggly and half covering her face. Her blue eyes blinked, wet with tears, then became covered with strands of hair. She slid down the wall and sat, the small case on her legs. Flames licked at the repaired door and spread toward the wall. Gunshots surrounded her, and she stared at the porch floor clutching the case.

Shot and yanked off their mounts to slam on to ranch dirt, nesters bled from the head, the belly, the chest, arms and legs. They did manage to shoot a few vigilantes. Mostly their weapons dropped and they cried and yelped in pain. The vanguard of them began to run, to ride back to their homes. The vigilantes were merciless. Even when down the men were shot through the head or the heart, whatever it took to end their lives for good. Faces of the shooters under the brim of low-pulled hats looked sharp and hard and frozen with determination – not hate, for hate required an emotion as deep as love or terror. There was no emotion, no hatred, just a dedication to clear the area of human debris, remove obstacles, stop movement, as if they were shooting a path through a buffalo herd, requiring no more thought than to just get the job done and move on to the next.

Leading the killing wave was Ward Cameron.

Hawkstone intended to dismount and help Caroline away from the burning ranch house. Joe Coslet was already there, off his horse and leading her away from the main house. Then Hawkstone saw Cameron jerk his horse around, and all other thought left him. He fired and missed. Cameron saw him and returned fire, the bullet whipping Hawkstone's shirt sleeve. Cameron heeled his sharp spurs into his horse and took off at a full gallop north, away from the burning buildings and the dead and dying men, in the direction of the retreating nesters. Hawkstone urged the buckskin in pursuit.

The killing and the burning ranch noise faded behind, and only the pounding hoofs of the buckskin reached Hawkstone. The fresh-reloaded Peacemaker was still in his hand. Cameron rode towards and between foothill rocks, yanking the reins, digging in his sharpened spurs, up towards the nester camp. Hawkstone fired – the gunshot echoed off canyon walls, the shot chipped rock close to Cameron. Cameron jerked the reins back, and in one smooth leg-swing swept out of the saddle. Leaning against a boulder the size of a stagecoach he aimed, paused, and shot Hawkstone. The bullet creased Hawkstone's side just under his armpit.

The shot was enough to spin him around, and the buckskin stumbled so he fell out of the saddle – he tightened his grip on the six-shooter, bounced, half rolled, then came up with the Peacemaker cocked still in his hand. He fired as

Cameron came racing towards him. The slug hit Cameron's gun hand and his Colt went flying. But by then he was close enough to leap at Hawkstone, and his fist knocked the Peacemaker between rocks. He backhanded Hawkstone across the face and swung his fists back and forth, striking cheeks, temple, side of the neck, just like at the creek and cut fence.

Hawkstone stumbled back and down, but he rolled and used another boulder to push to his feet. When Cameron came at him again, he jabbed his fists straight into Cameron's nose,. and kicked his knee. Cameron stumbled back and down, but quickly came up with a rock the size of a cantaloupe and hit Hawkstone on the forehead. Flashes and dizziness swept through Hawkstone's head and he staggered back.

Then Cameron bent to his boot and straightened with a ten-inch-bladed bowie knife in his hand. He swung the blade and sliced the back of Hawkstone's left hand. He leaned forward and jumped, but Hawkstone fell on his back and shoved his boots into Cameron's stomach and pushed him off. He spotted the Peacemaker stuck between rocks and rolled over to it.

Cameron jumped him and swung the Bowie down towards his chest. Hawkstone used his fist to strike the inside of Cameron's wrist, loosening his grip on the knife. Cameron rolled away, tightened his hold on the knife, then pushed to his knees. But by then Hawkstone had rolled to the rocks and got a grip on the Peacemaker and cocked the hammer. He spun to his back as the sharp blade came down towards his face. He fired two quick shots, and both slugs tore into Cameron's chest: the force of the bullets twisted Cameron to the side and the knife blade dug into green grass.

Hawkstone used the heels of his boots to slide his back up a boulder. Cameron blinked as his forehead fell to grass.

Apparently neither chest shot had pierced his heart. He turned his head just enough to look at Hawkstone. Hawkstone held the Peacemaker on his left leg, then lifted it.

'Damn you,' Cameron croaked.

Hawkstone shot him through the temple.

EIGHTEEN

With his blue kerchief pushed against the side wound under his shirt, Hawkstone mounted his buckskin and rode out of the rocks and east across the range towards the Circle-D. He saw no vigilantes, but knew they were ahead. Thinking Cameron was still alive they'd follow his instructions. They intended to hit the ranch before going after nester women and children. Already wagons from the nester foothill camp rolled towards the fire to pick up bodies and the wounded.

Hawkstone rode at an easy canter, peering ahead. As he rode close he saw the smoke.

Too late, he galloped on to the ranch yard. The remaining vigilantes had gone, looting whatever they could take from the ranch house. Evidently, word had reached them that Cameron was dead. Caroline was no leader, so without direction they took what they wanted from both ranches, and rode back to Cheyenne.

The bunkhouse and corral and part of the barn still stood. The ranch house, outhouse, tack room and barn smouldered as the last flames licked up from their foundations, now done with burning the wood-frame skeletons.

The wagon of women with two mules stood in front of the bunkhouse. The door was open. As Hawkstone tied the heavy-breathing buckskin to the hitch, he saw Millie's body inside on the main table. Willie Wink came out the door with his bowlegged walk, looking sombre. To Hawkstone's surprise, Brag Hailey, the bounty hunter, was with him, jamming his wrinkled, dirty Montana Peak hat on his head. He nodded.

Hawkstone returned the nod to both of them. 'Millie?'

'She's gone,' Willie said. 'Four of them vigilantes peeled off from the rest and swept through here like a river rapid, washed through with gunfire and torches and looting, then just as quick rode on out. Mebbe a stray bullet caught her.'

Brag looked back to the bunkhouse doorway. 'Seems there always got to be at least one innocent casualty.'

'They was caught up in the killing,' Willie said. 'They didn't care.'

Hawkstone stared at the bunkhouse. '*Evil knows it's ugly, so puts on a mask.*'

Brag turned to Hawkstone. 'That must be one of them Ben Franklyns. I suppose we got to hunt them down when we get the chance.'

Willie nodded. 'I brought the wagon in with the ladies right after, but they was gone and Millie was dead. Lindsey is beside herself, can't stop bawling. Nettie has her on one of the bunks. Yin Chun is giving her tea.'

Hawkstone turned to Brag.

Brag dug his toe in the dirt and pulled his hat brim down. 'I know you got questions, old pard.'

'Just one. Is Raines still walking among us?'

Hawkstone, Brag and Willie left the bunkhouse and went to the corral where they sat on the ground with their backs against a rail. Any warmth to the day faded as the sun dipped behind the Rockies. Brag had a bottle of decent drinking whiskey with no label, and a fresh pouch of Bull Durham. Hawkstone's was about empty. Ruth and Yin Chun had patched Hawkstone's side wound. They figured the hand scratch didn't need more than a strip of bandage. Willie had

96

a bullet crease across his forearm the women looked after. Done with fixing the men, they turned to preparing Millie for burial.

After lighting up, Willie said, 'Where did Joe get off to?'

'Out to the Bar-X,' Hawkstone said, 'or what's left of it. He's looking after her, the girl who owns it, Caroline Shelby.'

Willie squinted at Hawkstone. 'I thought her daddy owned it.'

Hawkstone shrugged. 'He's off prospecting in Alaska. She runs it, but he'll be real unhappy when he finds out the place is burned down and the special breed cattle are scattered over the horizon.'

Willie said, 'What about the Cameron fella?'

'He passed on from living.' Hawkstone turned to Brag.

'I know,' Brag said.

'Do I keep looking for him or is his body dumped in a marshal or sheriff office someplace?'

Brag took a long, deep drag on the smoke and let it out slow. He pulled a swallow from the bottle. 'The polecat doubled back on me. I figured him to keep on into the Black Hills, but he killed a pa and his daughter and come back on me. Dry-gulched me just outside Wounded Knee. I had some run-in with Kiowa too. But that little snake tried to pick me off with a brand new Winchester, and when that missed he sent two braves against me.' Brag handed the bottle to Willie. 'After I took care of the braves, I dumped some rocks down a hill on him and got close enough to wing-shoot him in the left shoulder.'

He shook his head, his hat all but hiding his face. He traced lines in the dirt with his finger. 'Should'a plugged the bastard right then, two in the chest, one in the head, dragged him to the nearest fort and claimed my reward.' He looked sideways at Hawkstone. 'Found out after, the reward is now three thousand.'

Hawkstone pressed his lips tight together. 'Be a crowd

after him for that amount.'

Brag dragged on the smoke while Hawkstone took a pull from the whiskey bottle. 'Old pard, I don't see how you'll get him all the way to San Francisco alive. You'll have to take back trails, you can't go the main roads, you'll get jumped for sure. That's if you catch him.'

'What was your last trace of him?' Hawkstone asked.

'Funny thing is, it was just outside Cheyenne. I wouldn't be surprised if he didn't show up here. He always had a hankering for that pretty little girl, Lindsey. And he's got money now. Gold taken from the two he shot down and money he got selling livestock, saddles, guns and anything else he took from them.'

Willie said, 'I don't think Lindsey will have anything to do with him.'

Brag shook his head. 'Oh, he's a sweet talker all right, can charm a girl right out of her unmentionables. He got to Lindsey once, likely figures he's got a worn trail there.'

'What he's got is a wounded shoulder,' Hawkstone said. 'And he doesn't know me.'

Brag sat straight. 'You never met?'

'He figures somebody is coming after him, besides you, but not who it is. Now, it'll be too crowded for him to tell them in pursuit one from the other.'

Brag rubbed his three-day whiskered chin. 'Come to think on it, I ain't ever been introduced myself, except for throwing rocks and lead. He ain't exactly anyone I care to know. But then none of them "Wanted" poster gents are.' He mashed the spent smoke under his boot heel.

Hawkstone flipped his cigarette across the yard. 'The poster money is waiting in San Francisco for you, Brag, with a bonus if you help me get him there. We'd have to fight off a few bounty hunters.'

'That's a long way, old pard, and he's slippery as an icicle.'

'I don't want you and me to tangle hat brims over it.'

Brag rolled forwards and stood. He brushed off his Levi's and took steps away from the corral, and turned back. He looked at Willie. 'What are *you* gonna do after this?'

'Collect my little Nettie and head on out for Oregon. We can't homestead no more but we can still buy land in the Willamette Valley for a buck-and-a-quarter an acre.'

'You want to help me gun down a murdering outlaw, I'll split the reward with you. You and Nettie can set off with fifteen hundred dollars.'

Hawkstone pushed to his feet and unhooked the thong holding his Peacemaker hammer as he faced Brag Hailey. 'You intend to draw down on me?'

'Not if I don't have to.' Brag moved his feet slightly apart. 'I know you ain't no gunslinger.'

'I'm not. And I don't want talk against what I got to do.'

Willie also stood up. He stepped between the two men, standing several inches shorter than both, and faced Brag. 'No, Brag. I ain't throwin' in with you. I won't go against Hawkstone, not after all he done for Nettie. I don't want you to brace him neither.'

'I sure don't want to.' Brag grinned at both of them. 'Don't know why we're fussing so much. We ain't even caught the slippery weasel yet.'

NINETEEN

Millie was buried out back in the family plot. Lindsey's red face shined wet with her tears. The few still at the Circle-D attended the burial where Hawkstone said a few words about how folks lived between the eternities, something he might have remembered from Ben Franklyn but he wasn't sure. After the cross was stuck in the earth, Brag rode out. The three cowhands still there pressed Lindsey about their future. She paid them off from the hidden cashbox, and they saddled up for Cheyenne. She gave Willie a month's pay.

Ruth Bowers approached Hawkstone as he dragged his packs from the wagon. She wore a dark blue dress, tight at the waist, the nearest she came to funeral black. Her close-set, nut-brown eyes searched his face. 'The side giving you some bother?'

'Yes'm. But it won't slow me much.'

'You're determined to hunt down this boy, this Raines fellow?'

'Brag already went to Cheyenne. He's got the jump on me, though I don't figure the weasel will linger there.'

Hawkstone slid the packs out over the lowered tailgate one by one and dropped them on the ground. He grimaced with side pain and rested. Willie and Nettie came from the bunkhouse, soon followed by Lindsey and Yin Chun. The grey mare stood docile while Hawkstone strapped the pack frame to her back. The buckskin was saddled and tied to a corral rail.

Willie helped lift one of the packs, and held it while Hawkstone tied it down. 'I wonder what happened over to the Bar-X? Joe is still there. You figure he lit out after the outlaw killer?'

'Mebbe,' Hawkstone said. 'Last I saw he was with the woman, Caroline. Her ranch house was burning down around her.'

Ruth glanced around at the other women, then at Hawkstone like she had something to say. 'We're heading out, Anson. Going for Fort Laramie and find a wagon train on the Oregon Trail. I want Lindsey to come with us. You too.'

'You got Willie, Ruth. You don't need me.'

'Just for a bit,' Ruth said. 'Help us get hooked up with a train.' She looked at him with intent. 'Be better if you stayed with us. Willie says the California Trail peaks southwest out of Fort Hill once we reach Oregon Territory.'

Willie stepped up. 'I was on that trail. It goes along the Humboldt river, then to Downy Pass and down through the Sierras to Sacramento. It's good solid road from there to San Francisco.'

'It'll be popular,' Hawkstone said, 'crowded with bounty hunters. I got to go a smaller, less populated way.'

Ruth put her hand on his arm. 'Please?'

Hawkstone hefted another pack to the grey. 'I'll ride with you as far as Fort Laramie, help you find a wagon train. Don't know if you heard Brag, but once I find the outlaw I got to keep him mostly out of sight, off the main trails. Bounty hunters will be combing the landscape. I still ain't sure Brag won't drop the snake on sight.'

They looked up as a one-horse buggy pulled in front of the burned ranch house. A small man in a tight dark suit

101

wearing a derby and spectacles gave them a tight-lipped smile as he edged the horse to them.

'Barnaby Hump at your service, folks. Ah, yes, a fine morning, I'd be looking for Millie Kyle.'

Lindsey sniffled and blinked. 'You're from the bank.'

'Why, yes I am. Is Millie about?' He spent a minute staring at the burned ranch house. 'I heard about this. The Bar-X too. A shame. A real pity.'

Lindsey said, 'We just buried my ma. She got shot in the vigilante raid.'

The black stallion pulling the wagon shook his head.

Hump pulled on the reins. 'Whoa, settle there.' He squinted at Lindsey. 'Sorry for the loss of your ma, Miss Kyle. That makes the ranch yours, correct? Is there a place we can talk in private?'

'Right here is good enough.' Lindsey put her dainty handkerchief to her nose. Her blonde hair was tied back at her neck. She wore a black dress buttoned to the throat.

Hump looked at those gathered around the grey as Willie held another bundle for Hawkstone to tie down. 'Yes, very well, if you insist. I was out at the Bar-X yesterday. I believe Caroline – uh, Miss Shelby – told me she was coming here. We – that is, the bank – made her an offer for the ranch that she accepted.'

'And that's why you're here?' Lindsey asked. 'To make me an offer?'

'Well, yes. However, there have been obvious changes.'

'Last time Ma was in your bank the offer was two hundred thousand.'

Hawkstone tied the pack rope tight. He looked up at the buggy. 'But that ain't the offer now, is it?'

Hump frowned at Hawkstone. He leaned toward Lindsey. 'Like Caroline, you've been burned out. You have few cattle still on the property. Any good grass grows in patches. Basically, except for the raw land, there is no ranch.' He pulled off his spectacles and cleaned them with a kerchief and put them back on. He patted his dark suit breast pocket. 'I have here a bank cheque for seventy-five thousand dollars, substantially more than I paid Miss Shelby – Caroline.'

Without hesitation, Lindsey said, 'I'm sick of this life and this place. I don't want no cheque. You give me seventy-five thousand cash or gold and I'll take it.'

Hump blinked hard enough to make his dark eyes shine. 'Let me assure you, Lindsey, our bank cheques can be cashed anywhere.'

Ruth stood close to Lindsey. 'Lindsey, you're coming to Oregon with us. You'll have a stake to get settled. You're coming. Say it.'

Lindsey took a full minute to stare at Ruth. She looked at Nettie and Yin Chun and Willie. 'Yes,' she said.

Ruth turned to Hump. 'You get back to the bank, you wire Fort Laramie and tell them a wagon is coming in with a young lady wants to cash one of your cheques. You say in that wire for them to have the gold – not cash – gold, ready.'

'I will,' Hump said with enthusiasm. He sighed. 'Is there anywhere private we can take care of the paperwork?'

'The bunkhouse,' Lindsey said.

Willie looked up towards the west. 'Wagon coming.'

Hawkstone was tying the last bundle on the grey. He saw a small prairie schooner pulled by two strong chestnuts with Joe Coslet at the reins. Caroline Shelby sat beside him wearing tight buckskin pants and a yellow linen blouse with a brown wool vest, her hair tied together at the back of her brown plains hat.

With the banker and Lindsey in the bunkhouse, Joe stopped the wagon, handed the reins to Caroline and stepped down. She looked at the eyes of the women standing in front of the burned house. Her gaze passed over the charred skeleton.

'What happened here?' she asked.

103

Ruth stepped to the wagon. 'Millie was killed by vigilantes. My name is Ruth Bowers. We're all headed to Oregon Territory.' She nodded to the others. 'The girl on the crutch is Nettie White. She was taken by Kiowa but it don't mean nothing to us. The young man there, Willie, likes her. Yin Chun is our mother-to-be. You're welcome to join us, Caroline.'

Caroline frowned. 'Join you?'

'Yes,' Ruth said. 'We know your story and we want you along.'

Caroline looked at each in turn. 'Much obliged.'

Once down from the wagon, Joe Coslet had gone to Hawkstone. 'I'm coming with you.'

'With me, where?'

'To gun down that murdering outlaw killer what cut my brother's throat.'

Hawkstone stood tall. 'There ain't going to be no gunning down. I told you all, I got to take the weasel to San Francisco pretty much intact. He can be shot up a little but he can't be killed.'

Joe pulled his hat brim down. 'I ain't sure that will set with me. I figure we might have to shoot us some vigilantes in Cheyenne along the way.'

'That ain't in my corral. I just got one thing to do. I might ride along with Willie and the ladies as far as Fort Laramie and get them set up with a wagon train. But then, I cut a trail on my own to find the bastard and haul his living carcass out west.'

Joe squinted with tight lips. 'To what?'

'According to my sea captain pard, Raines has a future lined out for him that will be more horrible than the vilest slaughter any savage might give him. And it's for the rest of his life. But he has to stay functional to live through it. That's my job.'

'He's got to pay for Al.'

'He will,' Hawkstone said, 'and for all them others.'

TWENTY

The Oregon Trail strung past the adobe and wood wall surrounding Fort Laramie. Currently along the Trail rolled five wagons originally from Missouri. Web Troop was the wagon master Hawkstone contacted, and he welcomed two added wagons. Most carried families with one or two small children. Hawkstone noticed the usual prejudice, especially from the wives, over Nettie White, a savage captive, and Yin Chun, a girl in a family way without wedlock.

Caroline and Lindsey became close and kept to themselves. They acted standoffish, as if they were better than the others, having once been ranch owners. But they would outgrow that. Ruth was the catalyst to keep everybody together. Being oldest she gave chore assignments and looked after Nettie's healing leg. She told Hawkstone that once established on the Trail, the wives would come around, especially when they saw how sweet the young women were.

The seven wagons had circled outside the fort. On a bright Monday morning, Hawkstone decided to say his good-byes to the ladies. He had heard nothing from Brag, and he hoped the killer outlaw they were both after was still somewhat alive. He reckoned after he'd left the ladies he'd head back to Cheyenne and ask some questions.

Next to a creek running south of the fort and circled wagons, Hawkstone sat on the bank sharing a smoke and a bottle with Web Troop to get a measure of the man. Web dressed cowhand, like he had punched trail cattle at one time, years ago. He wore a black flat-top hat, dusty and torn and sweat-stained, and Levi's jeans and a blue flannel shirt covered with a buckskin vest. A red kerchief circled his neck, and his creased face showed he had known hardship, hunger, hate and killing, and maybe love at one time. His small green eyes were almost hidden from years squinting against the sun under the wide brim of his hat. He carried an old Smith & Wesson six-shooter in a side holster with a rawhide loop over the hammer.

Web handed the bottle to Hawkstone while he rolled a smoke. 'Hawkstone: seems I heard that name. An army scout as I recall. Down in New Mexico and Arizona territories.'

Hawkstone took a pull from the bottle. It was cheap stuff and burned hard going down, but he welcomed the bite even on a Monday morning. He didn't like saying good-byes, especially to women he'd come to like. It twisted awkward in his chest. 'Yup, did that and a lot of other things. Looking for a bad *hombre* now, and thought to give you some warning.'

Web squinted at him. 'He figure to bother the lady wagons?'

'Could be. He got the Chinee gal in her family way, and now he's sweet on Lindsey.'

'Which one is she?'

'One of the blondes, the real pretty one.'

'I'll watch for him.' Web stared at the bubbling creek. 'Not much I ain't seen, Hawkstone. This will be my fourth trip along the Trail. The Trail's got deep wagon grooves in places now. Only the poor take it, most others use the train – still the best way to move household goods. But the train is too expensive for regular folks moving. Figure this trip, mebbe one more, and I'm done. I'm pushing past fifty now. The saddle wears me down. Gave up on having a woman

106

years ago. Had a Cheyenne squaw back in '61, went seven years 'fore she died of the fever. Best part of my life. She made me better than I ever was before or been since.' He shook his head. 'You don't get something like that twice in living.'

He took a pull from the bottle and handed it over, then he dragged deep on the smoke and flipped it in the creek. 'All I got left now, a good steak sometimes, some whiskey and Bull Durham. When I got the spare cash, I get myself a poke, try to get a pretty one, but that ain't always possible. Don't even get in saloon fights no more. The old bones won't take it.'

· Hawkstone said, 'Mebbe that's the future for most of us old trail drovers, though I got me a good woman now. She tends to spoil me.'

'Then what you doing here? You better be with her.'

'I will, soon as I find and deliver this fella I'm after.'

Next to Ruth's wagon, the watered and fed buckskin and packed grey waited. Hawkstone sat on a wooden box and finished off his ham and beans, washed down with tea, served to him by Yin Chun. He smiled looking at her with her protruding belly while she cleaned plates, her single braid straight down her back. Yin Chun and her Chinese tea. The cure for all ailments and pain. Tea was good for now. He'd have a trail loaded with coffee good and bad, soon enough. Nettie moved from the other wagon leaning on her crutch, entwined on Willie's arm. Willie looked at her with love, likely not even noticing the nose tattoos. Her face beamed like an angel, or at least a young girl in love. At the back of Ruth's wagon, Joe and Caroline stood forehead to forehead in quiet, intimate talk. Another romance starting. Lindsey washed dishes and Ruth dried.

Hawkstone watched them. They looked well entrenched in wagon-wheel life already. He handed the empty plate to

Lindsey for the wash tub. 'Well, folks, guess I'll be drifting along. I wish you well in Oregon.' It didn't sound right and he knew it. He didn't know what to say. Mount up and ride out.

Ruth gripped the hand towel while she went to him, a frown on her face. 'No, sir, Anson Hawkstone. You don't just say farewell and ride on out. Come here.' She wrapped her arms around his neck and pulled him close to her. 'Thank you for all you did for us.'

Yin Chun was next to grab him. She couldn't stand as close but she kissed the side of his neck. 'You our mighty hunter, Anson Hawkstone.'

Joe shook his hand in a hard grip. 'I oughta be coming with you.'

'I'll get him for you, Joe,' Hawkstone said.

Then tiny, petite Nettie was pressed against him in his arms. 'Thank you for my crutch, and so much more.'

Willie shook his hand.

No hugs from Caroline and Lindsey. He reckoned he hadn't done much for them. From the back of the wagon they gave him a nod and a smile.

Ruth said, 'You change your mind, you come on out Oregon way. Ask about us. We'll be easy to find.'

'Yes'm,' Hawkstone said. He swung into the saddle with a slight stitch in his side. He blinked hard as he walked the buckskin away from the circled wagons, towing the grey behind.

A Ben Franklyn came to him: '*Be slow in choosing a friend, slower to change.*'

TWENTY-ONE

Linus Raines didn't know how long he could stay with Molly
Bee in her downtown Cheyenne hotel room without half the
town finding out. Molly was a gregarious, friendly little gal
who had armies of friends in the hotel, the restaurant, and
working upstairs in one of the saloons. It was no surprise
when she burst into the room out of breath.

'He's here,' she said. 'He knows about you.'

No need to ask how the bounty hunter found out. They
seemed to be everywhere. 'What's this one's name?'

'Brag Hailey.'

Linus stared at the window. 'He dogged me up in the
Dakotas. I thought I dropped him on the trail someplace. Is
my horse saddled?'

'Waiting in the stable.'

Linus looked Mollie up and down. She was a wisp of a
woman, not much to her, no bigger than a minute. Not yet
thirty, her tiny face, now flushed and scrunched with excitement, was an oblong that was framed by her raven hair. The
hair went up, out, and down and had a pretty red ribbon on
the top of it. She pushed out the top of her red dress bodice
as if proud of what little she showed.

Linus had his saddle-bags and bundle over his left shoulder. He swept her into his right arm and kissed her in a way
he considered was as good as she deserved. 'Want to come

with me?'

She stepped away. 'Lord, no, honey. You got nothing ahead of you but trouble. I got friends. I got a life. Gentlemen give me nice jewellery and feed me. No way I'd be bumping on a horse along some trail with you. And you got men want you dead.'

'Think of the adventure.'

'The hell with that, honey. I don't need that kind of adventure.'

Linus patted her on the bottom. 'Go check the hallway and lobby, make sure the way is clear.'

'Sure, honey.'

When Mollie left the room, Linus loosened the strap of his saddlebags. He went to the dresser and opened the jewellery box, and without hesitation, dumped the contents into one of the bags; he then closed it quickly, and tossed it over his shoulder as Mollie came back in. He met her at the door and they went down the stairs together.

On the way to the stable, Linus said, 'When I get down to south Texas I'll send you a wire. Mebbe you can come visit.'

'That is if you're going to Texas.'

'OK, then come with me along the Oregon Trail. Lots of trees and gurgling creeks and majestic scenery.'

'You got a better chance getting kicked in the head by a longhorn, honey. I ain't leaving here, 'specially to go into some tumbleweed-blowing wasteland – or to freeze my skinny bones up there in the Rockies. No, honey, this is good-bye, and likely from now on.' At the stable she kissed him lightly, turned and walked her tiny body away from him.

Linus figured it wouldn't take long for her to find that empty jewellery box, so he figured he'd better mount and ride while he was able. Of course he had no intention of riding to Texas, at least not yet. He'd heard of the wagon train. Maybe the part about the Oregon Trail that he'd told Mollie Bee might be true – the wagon train rolling west carried some women he knew, especially a real pretty blonde.

Linus had to travel light and fast if he was to catch the wagon train out of Fort Laramie. He kept the young sorrel mainly at a fast trot, resting it often. After the rest he kicked it to a gallop for a few miles, then slowed to the trot. The wagon train would be moving slow. The trail kept climbing, and him with it. He had to unwrap his buffalo coat because as the sun went down, the air turned chilly. The upper Rockies were often dusted with snow, even in July. And this was only June.

The first village he came through he tried to sell a diamond locket. The village was poor. All wagon trains had to come through along the one main road. Residents scratched a living from trade with folks rolling their wagons, who had little money to start with themselves. Linus didn't need the money. He wanted to find out if the trinkets were genuine. They were. A jeweller at the general mercantile booth gave him $160 for the locket, probably half or one-third its value. But he knew flaunting jewellery around called attention to himself. For that reason, he moved the two-shot .32 derringer-type weapon from its vest pocket under his armpit to the saddlebag holding the jewellery, where it came to hand easily when he reached in.

The village consisted of the general mercantile that carried almost everything known to civilization, from cheap whiskey to used ploughs left behind to lighten the wagonload in the high Rockies, and had booths for traders like the shifty-eyed jeweller. Beyond that were a sagging hotel with ten rooms, two saloons named #1 and #2, a stable with a blacksmith who would fix broken wagon wheels and replace horseshoes, and a townhouse converted to a tired pleasure palace with tired pleasure women. They didn't have much trade from the wagons, who were mostly families, but there were enough hangers-on to keep house business brisk.

Not only did the house have hangers-on, but the village did too, from all economic and social levels, from slowing gunfighters to old codgers cadging drinks to feed the habit they couldn't shake. Pickpockets, thieves, robbers, back stabbers and murdering dry-gulch polecats slunk through the village following the wagons. Word of saddlebags loaded in stolen jewellery might be listened to with great interest.

The wagons would be heading for Yellowstone Country, then maybe swing down towards Boise. Linus figured to catch it within the next day or two.

Linus had an early dinner. The sorrel was frisky when he came out the bat-wing doors after a snoot-full of decent bourbon in Saloon #2. He led the horse towards a dark narrow alley between the hotel and a clapboard warehouse. After boarding the horse, he'd get a good night's sleep and ride out in the morning after breakfast. He was about to step into the stirrup when he saw a shadow in front of him.

'Keep both hands on the saddle horn.'

The man stood close on the other side of the saddle, a large revolver pointed at Linus's face. His black plains hat was silhouetted against street lantern lights at the ends of the alley. He wore all black, and looked like a gambler with a grand black moustache.

Linus stood without moving, both hands on the saddle horn. 'I got nothing you want.'

The stranger stepped closer. 'On the contrary, my friend, I disagree. Look at this moment as a crossroads. Whatever your life has been up to now is gone forever. What happens in the next minute will mark your thought and action for all the days – or minutes – you have left in this life.'

'What do you want?' Linus already knew what he wanted.

'We're standing in a dark alley, just the two of us, street lamps showing only enough illumination for us to see each other. We've had supper and a few drinks. Except for the tinkle from the piano in Saloon #1 we stand in silence. We can hear each other's boots grind in the dirt. What do you think I want? I'll be relieving you of your saddle-bags.'

'Nothing in them to interest you.'

'Again, I disagree, sir.' He took one step closer. 'We should have more light. Why do you look familiar? Have we met before?'

Linus began untying the bags. 'I don't think so.'

'You came from Cheyenne?'

'And parts north-east.'

'No, I've seen your image. Where? Where have I seen your face before?'

Linus had the bags untied. He left them straddled behind the saddle. 'You ain't seen it.'

'What is your name,' the robber asked.

'You're robbing me. You don't need no more.'

'Slide the bags on to the saddle. Unstrap one of them, the one with the most trinkets.' He stood rigid. 'Wait a minute. I believe there is a "Wanted" poster out on you. Three thousand dollars as I recall, dead or alive. You're that Linus Raines, outlaw killer.'

Linus unfastened the strap on the bag with the jewels. He slid his hand in, got a good grip on the Derringer, and shot the man through the bag into his nose. The robber jerked. He stood still for a few seconds. He looked to his left. His legs wobbled. He turned back, stared at his gun hand as if his effort should be to cock the hammer back.

Linus quickly drew his hand from the bag and immediately pulled his Colt .45, and shot the man twice again through the neck and chest.

The robber dropped his revolver. He fell to his knees, paused, then his face dropped straight to the dirt.

Linus holstered the Colt. He fastened the bag, now with a small hole in it, then squinted, cocking his head, listening for any sound of shout or shot. He tied the bags down. He

113

would reload the hide-weapon later – he still had a second shot in it. Without another look at the man, he swung into the saddle and heeled the sorrel towards the edge of town – its back hoofs kicked the dead man's head hard enough to knock off his black hat. No hotel bed for Linus tonight: he would sleep on the trail chasing down the wagon train.

TWENTY-TWO

Somewhere along 16th Street, downtown Cheyenne, up the road from Crow Creek, at high noon, Hawkstone entered the Half-Broke-Horse Saloon, which sat next to an imposing two-storey brick brothel with a full-length upper-storey balcony. He looked for Brag Hailey, who was supposed to introduce him to a woman named Mollie Bee. Brag had a good-sized glass of beer on the table, with another for Hawkstone. They nodded to each other as Hawkstone sat between Mollie and Brag. The saloon was populated with drovers from the herd that had just come up from El Paso through Indian Country. Mollie was a cute little package almost busting out the top of her bright green dress. She had milky-smooth skin and a quick smile, and wild dark hair with a red ribbon on top.

Brag said, 'Mollie Bee, this is my pard Anson Hawkstone. He ain't no bounty hunter like me. He wants the polecat for personal reasons.'

Hawkstone put his elbows on the table. 'What can we get you to drink?'

Voices rose in volume around them. Boots scraped the unpainted pine floor that had cracks between planks which sometimes caused chair legs to stick. An argument between two drunk drovers started at the bar. A tray was spilled, glasses broke. One man hit another, knocking him over a table, spilling drinks.

Mollie strained her neck to see the bar. She caught the bartender's attention and raised her hand. 'It's all right. Curly Bill is working. He knows what I want, he always does.'

Brag turned to Hawkstone. 'How come you wouldn't meet us at the *Green Elephant?*'

'Had a run-in with the owner there.'

'Over what?'

'He insulted our ladies. I threw a drink in his face and busted him one. Broke his gold eye-tooth, and slipped out a side door.'

'You should'a just shot him dead.'

'Too noisy, with too much attention. His insult wasn't serious enough to die over.'

A tall thin waitress slapped hands away as she brought Mollie a fat whiskey on a tray. 'Curly Bill says, hello. Be four-bits, gents, now.'

Hawkstone dropped a dollar on her tray along with a smile that was not returned.

Mollie nodded as the waitress left, the waitress pushing away a new gauntlet of hands grabbing at her. Mollie sipped her drink and turned to Hawkstone. 'The bastard stole my jewels, every last piece. Had his fun with me then took all my fortune without a by-your-leave.'

'To go where?' Hawkstone asked.

'He tried to convince me it was Texas, but he was with me four days, and a couple times he mentioned a pretty blonde hooked up on a wagon train. I figure he's on the Oregon Trail giving trinkets to her. I'll tell you what I want.'

Brag sat stiff and gripped Hawkstone's arm. 'There they are. Just walked in, them four.'

Hawkstone frowned. 'Who?'

Mollie said, 'You're not listening to me? Why you boys looking at them vigilantes?'

Brag put his hand on Mollie's. 'Vigilantes my Aunt

Matilda's bloomers. Them is cold, hard killers and they shot down a ranch owner lady friend of ours and burned all she owned. Seems like anybody can call themselves vigilantes these days. Me and Hawkstone got business with them four. We'll be getting back to you shortly.'

'What business?' Hawkstone asked.

Brag squinted at the four men walking to the bar and leaned to Hawkstone. 'They bragged on it after, pard, that's how I come to find how it all played out. After the gunfire at the Bar-X, a bunch of nesters and five vigilantes was dead. The rest decided, the hell with this and turned to ride back to Cheyenne while nesters collected their dead and wounded. All but four. Them four. They rode east, direct for the Circle D. They shot down three ranch hands in a gun fight, shot Millie Kyle dead, looted and burned the ranch and rode out leaving three bodies. The three ranch hands who survived buried their pards afore everybody found Millie.'

Hawkstone said, 'We can't kill them in here.'

'I figure to back-shoot them on the way out by Crow Creek.'

'No back-shooting.'

'They bragged on it, Hawkstone. Stealing and burning and killing, and they bragged on it.'

'We'll take them to the creek and shoot it out with them.'

Brag sighed. 'You ain't no quick-draw gunslinger.'

'No, I ain't.'

'Then get that Peacemaker in your hand now so you'll already have it handy.'

A surprise for Hawkstone was that the four men were small. It seemed to be that way with professional gunslingers. Few appeared to be tall or big men. Drunk cowhands ignored them as the four were marched at gunpoint out of the saloon the side way and down towards the creek and beyond to the noisy, smelly stockyards. Hawkstone had two of their guns, Brag the other two. One of their guns showed seven knife carvings in the grip.

'That's far enough,' Brag said. He dropped his two guns on the grass-covered ground close to a stockyard fence. He nodded to Hawkstone who did the same. 'Since you fellas got us outnumbered, I'll holster mine and you four can do the same. We'll draw on my word.'

'What about him?' a buzzard-nose said.

'He ain't a fast-draw so he keeps it in his hand.'

'That don't hardly seem fair.'

Brag stepped forward. His Colt was in its holster. 'Fair? You want to talk about a young woman and her ranch and talk about fair? Holster your weapons.'

Except they didn't holster. They leaped to the ground and with six-guns in hand they rolled and fired. Hawkstone shot two of them in the head right away. It took a second for Brag to clear his holster, especially after a first shot chipped his calf and threw his leg out from under him. He shot one in the chest. Hawkstone finished off the fourth.

After the quick crack of gunfire and grunts of men being hit by bullets, Brag and Hawkstone stood silent. Cattle filled the corrals and bawled. Nobody seemed to be around. One of the vigilantes turned on the ground and raised his Colt. Brag shot him through the mouth, then stumbled and went down on his left knee.

'We better take care of that,' Hawkstone said.

'You know we got to get out of Cheyenne now, likely out of Laramie County.'

'We'll find out what Mollie Bee wants, then ride on out,' Hawkstone said.

In Mollie's hotel room at the Inter-Ocean Hotel, the young doctor had wrapped up Brag's calf – it turned out to be just a skin crease – while Brag drained half a bottle of whiskey.

Mollie told the doctor to say nothing, and pushed him out of the room with a warm, wet, meaningful kiss.

Hawkstone sat in a puffy parlour chair and stared at the floor. He had a vision of the four men dying, and it set uneasy with him. Brag reached out the bottle to him and he took it.

'Nobody else to do it, Hawkstone.'

'I know.'

'They gunned down Millie Kyle and burned most of the ranch.'

Hawkstone took a long pull from the bottle. He handed it back. 'Can you walk without a crutch?'

'Just a nick. Not a problem. And I can ride.'

'He'll be going after the wagon train.'

Mollie Bee stood in the middle of the room. 'Don't forget me. I'm in the room and you two fellas got to get me what I want.'

Hawkstone figured it was an engineering miracle she didn't come out of the top of that dress. She wasn't that well endowed, but she showed most of what she had. 'We got an idea what that is.'

Mollie put her hands on her slim hips. 'I want one-third of the reward, one thousand dollars, and all my jewellery back.'

Brag grimaced as he moved his left leg. 'We're on our way to the stables. We can't come back to Cheyenne, not for a long time. Somebody will've found them fellas by now.'

'I can meet you,' Mollie said. 'I'll meet you in Fort Laramie after you deal with that sweet-talking snake.'

Brag pushed to stand. 'We may not find him quick. Mebbe my pard here wants a long conversation with him. Me, I plan to shoot him dead on sight.'

TWENTY-THREE

The jeweller in the village had a pelt of sandy hair over each ear, and spectacles. He watched nervously while Hawkstone palmed the locket. 'If that's stolen, as you say, I'm out more'n two-hundred dollars. How'm I gonna get that back?'

'You ain't,' Brag said. He limped to a rickety straight-back wood chair and sat down on it, rubbing the bandage around his calf.

'When?' Hawkstone asked.

The jeweller looked from one to the other. 'Yesterday, not sure exactly when.'

'Yeah,' Brag said, 'you get so busy after a wagon train rolls through. What's your name?'

'Horace.'

Hawkstone said, 'When did he ride out, Horace?'

Horace adjusted his glasses, keeping his eyes on the locket. 'I hear there's a reward out on the fella. I hear it's three thousand dollars. His name is Linus Raines. But you two fellas already know that.'

'You hear a lot, Horace,' Brag said.

Hawkstone dropped the locket in his vest pocket. 'When did he ride out?'

Horace's face wrinkled with the pain of disappointment. He stared at Hawkstone's vest. 'I got no idea. Hear he gunned down a tin-horn was mebbe trying to rob him.'

From the creaking chair Brag said, 'How did the tin-horn

120

know what the fella carried, that might be worth robbing? Did you have some talk with the tin-horn about the locket, mebbe offer to buy whatever the tin-horn found? You do that, Horace?'

'I wouldn't do that.'

' 'Course not.' Brag pushed up from the creaky chair. 'Let's ride, Hawkstone. He's got mebbe a day on us.'

Hawkstone glanced at Brag. He looked back at Horace. 'This village got a town marshal or a county sheriff?'

'Not likely,' Horace said. 'We just kinda take care of things ourselves. What about the two hundred and fifty I paid for that locket?'

At the mercantile door, Brag held it open while Hawkstone turned back. Two rough-looking drifters stood at the bar counter with whiskey glasses and a bottle. They pretended not to hear while they listened.

'Leave him with a Ben Franklyn, pard,' Brag said.

Hawkstone nodded. *'Experience runs a hard school, yet fools will learn from no other.'*

They stayed on the Oregon Trail riding hard, Brag on his roan, Hawkstone riding the buckskin. The horses ran well, both used to open range and trail riding, and knowing their riders. Hawkstone had sold the grey at Fort Laramie with his pack, figuring to buy replacements at Fort Hall in Oregon Territory before he branched off to Utah, Nevada and California. That would be after he had Raines hog-tied and docile. He still had to work out how to keep bounty hunters from dry-gulching him.

It was likely the wagon train had not reached the Rockies yet, but they had to be drawing close. Brag and Hawkstone slept two hours the first night, four hours the second. They fed their mounts a few oats they carried because they demanded much from them. Mostly, the horses ate range grass and drank creek and river water. The men lived on a small amount of smoked ham and beans. When that ran out, they shot rabbits. Anything bigger would not keep the way they rode.

The fourth night, after the rabbit had roasted on the campfire spit, when they were close to Independence Rock, Hawkstone knew they needed more sleep. They now skirted the edge of open range within the shadow of the Rockies. After supper they sat by the campfire sipping coffee laced with decent whiskey, and rolled their smokes.

Brag said, 'He's caught the train by now.'

Hawkstone nodded. 'We can't brace him, tired like we are. We got to sleep good tonight.'

'Mebbe he laid over in Independence Rock. He's riding that young sorrel, or mebbe something else he took from that pa and daughter he murdered up in the Dakotas. The sorrel is a fast stallion, and I bet the killer is running him hard. What you figure he'll do when he reaches the wagon train?'

'Take Lindsey Kyle. She's young, beautiful, and has all that ranch gold from the bank to buy something out in the Willamette Valley in Oregon. The lad will take his fill of her, then ride on. He's been there before.'

'Not if we get to him in time.'

The two men sat silent under a thin canopy of firs and pines listening to the crack and snap of the campfire. Hawkstone had something clawing at his insides he wanted out between them.

He flipped his spent smoke into the campfire. 'It's been out there but we ain't kicked it around to a finish.'

'I know,' Brag said. 'There will only be one finish. I'll shoot the bastard down on sight and collect the reward. I ain't gonna fight a crowd of other bounty hunters trying to turn him in alive. He ain't worth dying over.'

'I told you, help me get him as alive as we can to San Francisco and the reward is waiting, with a bonus. My shipmate has the money, and he'll pay it gladly. But the weasel has got to be breathing and moving around on his own.'

Brag used a tree limb to stir fire coals. 'You know how many bounty hunters there'll be between here and San Francisco? A promise of three thousand dollars will bring them out of every saloon and whorehouse.'

'We'll stay to small trails, avoid the main roads.'

Brag stared at the resurrected flame. 'This shipmate of yours must be a very good friend.'

'He is. We spent eight years sailing the world together. The lad we're after did his daughter rotten and his punishment has to be long and hard – life-ending long and body-tearing hard. Dying by gunshot is too quick and painless.'

Silence spaced between them. Breaking it, besides the crack of the fire, the wind above rustled tree branches and needles.

'I'll think on it 'til we get there,' Brag said. 'We don't know what we'll ride into. Could be you and me got no say how events play out.'

'I'm turning in,' Hawkstone said. He felt bone-weary tired. He stretched out with his saddle for a pillow.

Brag was already stretched and covered as the flames played down to embers again. He coughed and spat on the other side of the embers. He was silent for a spell, then said, 'I need that three thousand, Hawkstone. I ain't had bounty money in almost six months. That's a long stretch without much income. I know my way of life is fading. I got no talent for nothing else.'

'You got no competition from me, Brag. I'm not interested in the bounty.'

'I know. You ever think on how we're losing our way of life? Look at the Oregon Trail. Since the railroad come, it's turning to weeds. Weeds, and deep, mud-filled ruts. The only folks who use it is families that need all their stuff with them. Not much homesteading out in Oregon Territory no more. They got to buy the land now. And you and me, every place we go we see encroaching crowds, towns, paved streets, street lamps, and them damn wire fences. We got little open space any more.'

'Plenty of space, Brag. We just got to go where it is. Oregon and Washington Territory has plenty. A man can venture up to Canada. Still lots of southern prairie in the New Mexico and Arizona Territories. But you're right. Us and the Indians. Fellas like you and me are getting pushed out with advance settling. We're running out of free space. The land is becoming homes for families moving west to live and grow. We got to change or perish. More important, the Indians got to change or perish.'

Brag spat again. 'Mebbe it'll be easier for them than us.'

TWENTY-FOUR

Brag Hailey and Anson Hawkstone caught up to the wagon train the next night. It had started the steep climb and was almost to Independence Rock, circled in a mood of fear and foreboding.

'He threatened and done some shooting,' Web Troop told Hawkstone. 'Wounded two men. Caught me in the left arm, not too bad, but I ain't a hundred per cent. He took a horse and got the Kyle girl on it and rode off.' His lean face wrinkled with anxious excitement in the glow from the centre of circled wagon campfire light.

Hawkstone had himself surrounded with Ruth Bowers holding his arm and Nettie on her crutch and Yin Chun close by. Caroline Shelby and Joe Coslet were not to be seen.

Willie Wink stood in front of Hawkstone close to Nettie. 'I was going after him but I worried on Nettie. He might get rid of Lindsey and double back.' He slapped his thigh. 'I had a bead on him, had him right there in my sight. I should'a dropped the bastard where he stood.' He tipped his hat to Nettie. 'Apologize for the bad language, my darling.'

Ruth looked up at Hawkstone's face. 'You look worn.' She turned to Brag. 'You both do. You need rest and something besides trail food, something a woman cooks for you. Good coffee.'

Yin Chun put her hand on Hawkstone's chest. 'I bring

you tea. It fix you good.'

Hawkstone stared at Web. He would know. There was no time for good food, friendly women and decent coffee.

'Northwest,' Web said. 'He started to steep climb right away, headed for Yellowstone Country.'

'How big a jump?' Hawkstone asked.

'Three, four hours. She fought him but he's got her tied pretty good.'

Brag had already swung up into the saddle, grimacing with leg pain.

Ruth clung to Hawkstone's arm. 'Anson, don't. Rest awhile.'

Hawkstone jumped his boot into the stirrup and swung into the saddle. He felt a stitch in his side. He pointed his finger at Willie. 'Stay with the train and back up Web.' He silently led the way out of the wagon circle and into dark forest.

They were used to life on the trail and they pushed their horses without rest, but they had to pick their way slow through mountain passes in the dark. Fresh horse droppings told them they were on the right trail. When they reached open stretches they galloped their mounts, Hawkstone stealing what moonlight he could to pick out signs – a spent whiskey bottle, broken branches, hoofprints in mud, a spent smoke, a torn piece from Lindsey's dress. While they rode they climbed, through rocky passes, along a small canyon. Hawkstone was concerned about ambush. There were caves within the rock faces, a few big enough to hide a pair of horses. Signs were fewer now because of the hard surfaces.

A few miles ahead lay Soda Springs. It might take the wagon train two or three days to reach it. Raines could try to by-pass the town. Riding so hard from pursuit didn't leave him much time to play with Lindsey. Hopefully she was

said how it will be.'

Lindsey blinked at him but remained still.

Raines gripped his saddle horn. 'She's been a head-pain since this started.'

'You're the one started it,' Hawkstone said.

Brag pushed his palm on the grip of his Colt.

Hawkstone moved slightly away from Raines. 'Swing your-self down from the saddle. I'd like it better if you were on your feet while I tie you. I'll just be helping myself to your saddle-bags.'

Silently, Raines leaned over the saddle horn and swung his right leg over the rump of the sorrel. As he eased down with Hawkstone watching, he pulled the derringer-type weapon from his vest underarm pocket, pushed the buck-skin's neck, aimed carefully and shot Brag Hailey through the heart. He swung the firearm to the right and fired again, but Hawkstone had bumped his buckskin against the sorrel, spoiling Raines' aim. The gunshot cracks snapped around the surrounding forest. The complaining crows cawed loudly as they flew high and away.

Lindsey screamed.

Hawkstone had the Peacemaker in his hand. He cocked and fired at Raines.

Raines spun once. His foot left the stirrup. On his feet, he stumbled a step, dropped the small two-shot and fell on his face to the rocks.

TWENTY-FIVE

At Soda Springs during late afternoon, Hawkstone checked Lindsay Kyle into the small hotel. He had buried Brag Hailey just outside Independence Rock. Linus Raines had taken a bullet into his chest near the heart. A kerchief and strips of Lindsey's petticoat were used to stem the bleeding and keep the wound closed. The bullet had lodged in a back rib, so nothing could be done on the trail. He sat hunched in his saddle tied down tight, and his sorrel was led to town where he was deposited with the local doctor.

Hawkstone stayed close by to keep him in sight.

The next day, the wagon train came through town to provision. The wagons brought light rain at first, then it poured for a full day. People and horses and mules rested, circled just beyond the stables. Hawkstone was spoiled with good food and hot tea and the company of pleasant women. He and Web Troop shared whiskey and smokes among the circled wagons. Raines was kept chained by the ankles to the doc's office, safe until he was healed enough for travel; the ankle chains connected him to a wagon wheel, and he was stretched on a blanket under Ruth's wagon, and was fed and given water to drink. The bandage was changed, but nobody talked to him.

After two weeks, flooded rivers and creeks subsided, and the wagon train was ready to move on. Hawkstone decided he would ride along with them the two-day journey to Fort Hall. Brag's roan was kept tied behind Ruth's wagon. He thought to put Raines in one of the wagons so his face was out of view. Looking at that face with its three-thousand-dollar reward caused Hawkstone to grit his teeth in hate. He missed his road partner, Brag Hailey, and did not look forward to trail miles with Raines. He decided not to let the killer feel the comfort of Ruth's wagon – he could ride his sorrel with the chain running from one ankle to the other under the horse. His hands would be tied to the saddle horn as he had tied Lindsey's.

The journey to Fort Hall went with only one incident. The overnight stay with circled wagons attracted a bounty hunter, who braced Hawkstone. He looked poor, with ragged clothing and a dirty tan, wrinkled plains hat. His brown mustang was old, and his Remington was pushed inside a scratched holster with worn tears at the trigger guard. He carried it cross-draw. He rode into the camp and dismounted without being invited. He looked hard at Raines under the wagon and the chain to the wagon wheel.

With the reins of the mustang in his hand he approached Hawkstone. He eyed the cup of tea Hawkstone had in his hand. 'Evening.'

Hawkstone said nothing.

'I got a poster.'

'You're too late. The outlaw is in custody.'

'You a marshal?'

Hawkstone sipped his tea. 'I'm the *hombre* got the outlaw in custody.'

'You taking him to Fort Hall?'

Hawkstone eased his palm to the grip of the Peacemaker. 'You ask a lot of questions. You come into camp, step down before anybody invites you. You don't introduce yourself, and you ask a lot of questions. If you're a bounty hunter, you're too late.'

131

'What if I said I'm a Federal Marshal?'

'You ain't,' Hawkstone said.

'You don't know that.'

'You got the trail-worn look of a bounty hunter. If you're a Federal Marshal, prove it.'

'I don't got to prove nothing to you. I figure to take custody of the outlaw.'

Hawkstone took another sip of tea. 'Or die trying.'

'How's that going to happen?'

Behind him, Web said, 'Mebbe 'cause I got a double-barrel twelve-gauge aimed at your spine. Mount up and ride on.'

The bounty hunter looked at the ground in front of him. Hawkstone watched his eyes. Did he really think he was fast enough? The gaze went from the ground to Hawkstone's face to the cup of tea in his hand, the Peacemaker, over to Ruth's wagon, the chains around Raines' ankles, back to the ground. He had to think it was all too much in too short a time. He nodded, turned, pulled his mustang close and creaked the saddle mounting. Without a word, he turned his mount and rode out of camp.

Web watched the mustang walk out of sight. 'You may have to kill that jasper somewhere on the trail.'

'Or half-a-dozen like him,' Hawkstone said.

Fort Hall had a massive log wall surrounding it. Gold prospectors used it as a gathering place for provisioning. The army presence was large, since the memory of the massacre of General Custer up in Wyoming Territory was still fresh. As they always do, politicians wanted answers. Now the questions came. How did such a thing happen? How *could* it have happened? The scouts knew, whom Hawkstone drank with. Some of these were Pawnee, or Cherokee or Cheyenne. Hawkstone did his drinking with them outside the fort while Raines stayed chained by the ankles, wrists and waist to a wagon wheel. Since Hawkstone's life was south in the Arizona and New Mexico Territories, he knew little details of the subject, but he did manage to gather some facts. Like most army generals left over from the war, Custer was self-centered and arrogant. But he wasn't stupid. What sealed his fate and that of the Seventh was ignorance of the conditions.

At no time in history had the army run up against more than a scattering of savages. Generally Indians ran in small bunches, but unknown to white eyes, the tribes had joined, many nations gathering together into one army, estimated at between 6,000 to 9,000 warriors. Coupled with that, the few hundred of the Seventh Cavalry consisted of at least one-third raw recruits with no Indian combat experience whatsoever, and all far too young to have fought in the Civil War. And there were many other contributing factors: scouts who turned on the army; brilliant tribal chief strategy; other army generals ignorant of the situation.

While Hawkstone enjoyed the banter of the scouts, after three days the wagon train was ready to move on, and so was he. He had wrapped the contents of Raines' saddlebags and addressed the package to Molly Bee, c/o Inter-Ocean Hotel, Cheyenne, Wyoming.

In Fort Hall, Hawkstone mailed the package. He traded Brag's roan for a big strong mule. The two that pulled Ruth's wagon had made him prefer mules to horses when it came to packing and hauling. He acquired a dark grey mule and a pack frame for everything he would need for the ride to deliver Raines to San Francisco. He also bought plenty of ammunition for the Colt and the Winchester.

Lately, being around the wagon train women, and the young love activity of Willie and Nettie, who took time for a small wedding ceremony at the fort, and the quiet intimacy of Joe Coslet and Caroline Shelby, Hawkstone kept thinking more and more about Rachel, the medicine woman. He had been away from her too long. While Ruth Bowers started to openly show affection for him, there was only one woman for Hawkstone, and he reckoned he ought to be getting back to her.

With the mule packed and Raines chained to his sorrel, Hawkstone said his goodbyes to the ladies among tears and hugs.

Web gripped his hand. 'You could ride on with us to Boise, then cut south.'

Hawkstone shook his head. 'Best if I head southwest now, skirt the California Trail, ease along the Humboldt, cut across Utah into Nevada, then the Downy Pass, the Sierra-Nevada over the Donner Pass and down towards Sacramento. I'll try to stay on secondary roads and trails.'

'Nasty desert to Verdi, Nevada. I rode it little over two months ago.'

Hawkstone smiled. 'Forty more miles of it beyond to Virginia City. The cockroach can use the punishment.'

Web put his hand on Hawkstone's shoulder and walked with him away from earshot to the others. He rubbed his gnarled hand across his mouth. 'You'll come to a water hole about fifty miles out from Virginia City. You'll see a shack, but the well is dry. You got to go north one mile to an under-ground stream. If you look real close you'll see a different colour in the sand, like the ground is moist, not wet, and you got to look hard. Might take some digging, go down almost a foot. The sand will fall away, and the stream is there to fill. Clear, cool water. Due north of the shack. Get your direction from the sun.'

Hawkstone nodded. 'Much obliged, Web.'

'You'll need it,' Web said. 'You'll be dry with thirst and be thinking you ain't gonna make it. An old prospector I run into told me about it. I was riding hard for Missouri on account of I had this here wagon train to Oregon job waiting for me. I knew I'd be late. Rode like the Pony Express. Wore out four horses.' He tipped his hat back on his sandy hair. 'You load up with water there and that'll get you to the Sierras, and on to Californy.'

Hawkstone left the wagon train, and the men and women he had befriended. Raines, the outlaw, rode last in line behind the buckskin and mule, the reins of the sorrel tied to the tail of the mule. A load of trouble had been left behind, but Hawkstone knew that much more waited ahead.

TWENTY-SIX

The second day on the trail, Anson Hawkstone knew the bounty hunter was dogging them. He also knew the man was determined, and would not leave them alone without a killing. He had been warned. No man should expect more.

The bounty hunter did not let him get clear of the Rockies.

At noon three days after leaving the wagon train, Hawkstone and Raines came down a pass into a rolling hill meadow between peaks about a mile long. The weather was sunny and warm. The road led straight down the middle about the width of a big Conestoga, with thick grass on each side. Recent rain had left puddles. Hawkstone started down the road then halted his small train. He sat his saddle with his head down, squinting, listening to the sounds around him. The buckskin pawed the ground.

'What is it?' Linus asked from behind him.

'Shut up,' Hawkstone told him.

'It's the bounty hunter, ain't it? Gonna dry gulch you and mebbe shoot me down. Perfect place for an ambush. Sure a place I'd choose.'

Hawkstone lightly heeled the buckskin. The three animals stepped ahead. He unfastened the rawhide loop on his Peacemaker. As the animals walked, he watched the brush along each side. When he saw a break, he turned right into it and continued with boot-high grass brushing past,

136

growing taller as he went. Ahead he heard the splash of a creek. The grass ended at a rocky bank where clear water gurgled gently over small rocks. He turned left and continued along the bank, horse and mule hoofs clomping over pebbles and small rocks. Ahead, he heard the quick movement of a trotting horse coming through the grass, across in front. The noise stopped around a bend in the creek out of sight. Another horse crossed the creek, hoofs splashing and sliding on rocks. A horse moved ahead on the same side as Hawkstone.

The bounty hunter had found a friend.

Hawkstone cleared his holster with the Peacemaker in his hand, the hammer cocked. He continued forwards.

Raines cleared his throat. 'Jesus, Hawkstone, don't make me a sitting target. I got no chance like this.'

Hawkstone said nothing while the buckskin stepped on. There would be killing in this tall grass, but he didn't intend it to be Raines. His gaze jumped along both sides of the creek and ahead at the curve. Grass grew horse-head high along the banks here where fresh water splashed constantly on it.

'Hey, Marshal!' a voice called out of sight ahead. 'You got a name, Marshal? Only you ain't no marshal, jest a regular fella like me.'

'His name is Hawkstone!' Raines shouted.

A short silence followed. Then, 'Hey, Hawkstone, did you hear? The bounty went up to five thousand. That's five thousand dollars for his worthless ass. Me? My name is Dexter. Dexter ain't hoggish, old hoss. I can share. That much bounty is a lot more'n I need. We can split it. What I'll do is help you guard the slick weasel on our way to the next marshal office. We divide the reward right down the middle. No need to kill him unless he gets sassy. What do you say, old hoss?'

Behind Hawkstone, Linus Raines shouted, 'I got gold,

Dexter. Lots of it. More than any bounty on me.'

He was lying, of course. The gold Raines had taken from the couple he had murdered was gone. Hawkstone had given most of it to Joe Coslet to help with the pain the outlaw had caused when he'd escaped, slicing Al's throat. The rest went to Willie and Nettie. There was no gold, no jewellery, nothing. Hawkstone wanted to remind him of that, but he thought he spotted Dexter through a break in the grass. Ahead, slightly to the left, the man bent over the saddle on the tired mustang, trying to hide, worn hat cocked, listening to outlaw lies. But the other one was across the creek where grass grew higher.

Dexter said, 'You sure 'nuff got gold? How much?'

'Look out!' Raines shouted.

Hawkstone fired two quick shots. Both hit Dexter in the side near the chest. He yanked up on the reins as he straightened and the mustang reared and stumbled back. He fired towards Hawkstone, but his aim was off. He moved forwards again to the grass break. High grass on the other side of the creek rustled as the second rider galloped ahead. Hawkstone shot Dexter in the head, then swung the Peacemaker towards the sound coming from his right, squinting to pin-point exactly where it was coming from. The horses jumped and swayed.

The second man was riding a big white stallion, and fired three times before he reached water. He wore a peaked white hat that swung and twisted while he searched along the creek. It gave Hawkstone enough time to shoot the hat, an arm, and the belly. The man jerked and twisted out of the saddle and splashed loud into the water. His gun hand lifted as if reaching for the sun, and the pistol dropped with a splashing plop. It would take an hour for him to die.

Approaching the Nevada desert, Linus Raines would not shut up.

'You sure enough taking me back to Frisco and that sweet little wife of mine, Hawkstone? That *is* your name. I heard others call you that. Captain Ben got my future worked out, I'll bet. Back with the little woman and my brat kid. Well, Martha is young, and she's got that perfect slim body I like so much. Only, there's the bounty.'

Hawkstone ignored his banter as they began their crossing of the burning desert.

'I know what the captain will do,' Raines said. 'He'll have Martha and me live in some exotic place in the world where the law can never find me. He has a fleet of ships, he can choose anywhere on the planet. It won't be a bad life. I don't mind, neither. That girl worships me. Ain't nothing she won't do for me. And I'm her husband, the father of her kid. All you got to do is make sure no bounty hunter fills me with lead before we get there. Think you can do that, Hawkstone? Your name is Hawkstone, right? Like I say, it's what everybody calls you. What you got to do with my father-in-law, Captain Ben? Why the hell won't you talk to me?'

Since the outlaw ignored orders to shut up, Hawkstone shoved a sock in the babbling mouth and put a pillow case over his head to keep from looking at him. The case kept his face from the view of any potential bounty hunters they came across along the way. When the case and sock were removed to feed and water the outlaw, his heated face was beet red and drenched in sweat. He complained that he certainly would die in the desert with likely infection in his chest wound and the hard way he was being treated. Hawkstone allowed that at this stage it didn't much matter one way or the other.

At the water hole fifty miles out of Virginia City they were hit again.

Three men rode towards the shack while Raines and Hawkstone ate pork and beans; the chain was moved to the outlaw's wrists, and rattled with each movement. The well outside the shack was dry. The shack walls had been broken out, and were used more for shade than shelter. They sat in shade on wooden boxes others had left.

Raines coughed and stared at Hawkstone. 'We ain't got more than two swallows of water between us. And fifty miles to Virginia City. What you gonna do now, Hawkstone? If that's your real name.'

Hawkstone squinted toward a shimmering horizon. 'Deal with the three *hombres* coming at us.'

Raines followed Hawkstone's gaze. 'More bounty hunters, you think? A five thousand reward is gonna make me honey-sweet to more gunslingers than you can handle. I guess I need you to keep me alive, so I can crawl beside my smooth, sleek, loving wife. She ain't never known no man but me, and I do make her smile.' He dropped his empty tin plate to the desert sand. 'I'll take a drink of water now.'

Three weary men rode up to the shack on stumbling, worn horses. They glared at Hawkstone out of bleary eyes, and touched tongue tips to scaly dry lips. Their shirts had soaked up sweat, then been dried by desert wind, then absorbed sweat again. Now the clothing looked crusty and sand tinted. The horses stopped at the shack, necks no longer able to keep their heads up. Each head moved low, mud-caked nostrils puffed to blow sandy dirt. The oldest of the three men, with white hair under his short-brimmed hat and a full silver beard, tried to sit tall in the saddle, without success. His glare passed from Hawkstone to the chained outlaw returning his stare.

'Mind sharing your water?' The old man's words came croaking with little moisture.

'The well is dry,' Hawkstone said.

The young man behind said, 'You're lying.'

'Step down and see for yourself.'

Instead, the young man also turned his glare to the chains.

The old man pressed his lips together. 'Linus Raines.'

The two young men behind reached for their weapons.

'Don't!' Hawkstone had his Peacemaker out and shot the young man on the right. He felt the slam of a slug crease his upper left arm muscle as the old man cleared his holster. He fell back over the box, flashing lights sparkled behind his eyes. He fired again at the two remaining and hit one, but he wasn't sure which. What felt like a hot poker singed his forehead above his left eye, as the crack of gunfire rolled across dry, empty desert.

The sparkles turned black, and he felt his face push against hot sand.

He heard Linus Raines scream.

TWENTY-SEVEN

A Ben Franklyn came as his first thought. '*There is no little enemy.*'

The sagging shack offered no shade from a rising sun, certainly none where Hawkstone was curled, his blood blotted around him by coarse, dry sand. As the sun crept higher, shade eased towards his boots and legs. His head pounded. His left eye was closed by dry blood. He shifted, and the sound of his body scraping sand echoed loud around him. He tried to swallow, but no moisture went down. Up on his elbows, he wiped his left eye and looked beyond the shack. Two men and three horses lay dead in the sun. Missing were his buckskin, the mule, the sorrel and Linus Raines. Four empty canteens were scattered around him. His Colt Peacemaker .45 was gone, along with all other weapons.

He reckoned his shot had missed the old man.

Sitting, he aligned the position of the sun, then looked north. Nothing was out there, a shimmering horizon and empty heat between. He hoped Web was right. He needed a weapon. Even his bowie knife had been pulled from its belt sheath. Moving made his head start to bleed again. It was a bullet crease, just broke the skin. The arm muscle was damp, but not flooding. He pulled his neck kerchief and wrapped it tight around his head. Questions that bombarded him just

142

worsened his headache, so he ignored them. Raines might be dead. The old man might have died a day's ride out. The two horses and mule were well fed and watered so they would still be plugging along. Or standing and waiting.

At first he had thought the two young men were related to the old timer, maybe his sons, but no longer. They were either hired, or just pards riding along looking for mischief. There was no resemblance to him.

Hawkstone pushed to his knees. Using one of the rickety support beams, he pulled to his feet. He fought dizziness until he was used to the height. He looked up at the pale blue sky that held a blistering white sphere of sun. Not one cloud could be seen. There should have been buzzards, but where would they come from in a land of snakes and lizards? He stumbled to begin his search of the bodies.

One of the men carried a loaded hideout back-up weapon, small calibre, maybe .32, a loaded one-shot; it was an odd shape, not like a Derringer, might have been foreign. Hawkstone searched for spare cartridges, but found none. The other man had a folding jack-knife in his jeans pocket, and a half-full Bull Durham tobacco pouch and paper in his silk vest pocket. Hawkstone used the knife to cut the man's calico shirt sleeve that he wrapped around his wounded left arm muscle. He rolled himself a smoke and lit up, but the smoke made his throat feel drier. Any money the two men had had was taken. And, of course, their holster guns.

At the shack he gathered the four empty canteens. Once more, he checked the position of the sun. He tried to think of a Benjamin Franklyn to fit the occasion, but couldn't. Those like the dead men, he had known many times before. The old man showed greed and evil, and he had many twins like him throughout the West.

Hawkstone had crossed deserts before. Nothing that had happened here was new to him. He felt the pain, but even that he had felt before. The dominant feeling he carried was

143

the concentration of pursuit. He would find and kill the old man, then deliver Raines to San Francisco, alive if he could.

He began to trudge to the north.

After finding the waterhole and filling the canteens, it took a day to find the old man and Raines. By then he had three full canteens; the fourth canteen was half empty. The old man trudged in the lead holding the buckskin's reins. Hawkstone came up behind them, sliding and stepping through hard, hot sand. The mule followed the buckskin, still tied to the saddle. Linus Raines drooped over the side of his sorrel, part of the chain across the seat. Only his wrists tied to the horn kept him from dragging along the desert. His head hung low enough to bounce now and then. He wore no hat.

The old man did not turn as Hawkstone approached. His left hand gripped the reins, his right, a six-shooter. The mule was the first to smell the full canteens. He tried to turn his head towards Hawkstone, and the jerk slowed the buckskin in front of him. Raines tried to lift his head as Hawkstone stumbled past and ahead to the pack carried by the mule. The guns were tied to the top. Hawkstone found and untied his Colt .45. He blew the sand off it, then stumbled along to the buckskin, where the old man heard him and finally began to turn.

The old man fired a wild shot, almost fell, let go of the reins and took better aim.

Hawkstone fired the Peacemaker twice quickly. One slug snapped the old man's head back, the second ploughed into his gut.

The revolver dropped and the old man followed, to his knees, then face down into hot sand.

Behind Hawkstone, Raines' scratchy throat whispered, 'Water. Hawkstone, water.'

*

There were few stops crossing the Sierras. Raines complained constantly and spent most of his awake life on the trail, gagged and head-covered. Another bounty hunter was shot dead just outside Sacramento along the banks of the big river. Three toughs lay in ambush at the San Francisco city limits. Hawkstone caught another bullet across his shoulder putting them down. Raines took a hot crease to mark his cheek.

But they reached the wild waterfront coast, and the harbour where all manner of boats and ships were built, from ocean-crossing clippers to skiffs to fishing vessels. By the time they rode into the boatyard, summer was all but gone, and it was raining.

Rain kept shipbuilder carpenters home. In the deserted yard, Hawkstone fell more than stepped down from the buckskin. He unlocked the chain and untied Raines, and pulled him from the sorrel. The rain poured down harder, making him shiver. He gripped the outlaw killer's collar and dragged him across the yard and up the stairs and into the ship-building office of Captain Ben Coral. Ben was leaning over a drafting table, but spun around when Hawkstone bounced with a crash to open the door. Shoving Raines to the floor, Hawkstone felt a wave of dizziness.

'My God, Anson,' Ben said. 'Martha, get somebody to fetch the doctor.'

'There he is,' Hawkstone said, his voice raw, barely a whisper. 'Shot up some but alive, mebbe more than me.' He stumbled back against the wall and let the dizziness overtake him. He faded to unconsciousness as he slid to the floor.

TWENTY-EIGHT

A letter was written to Rachel, the medicine woman, telling her Anson Hawkstone would soon be on his way home. He had some more healing to do. The sweet daughter of Ben Coral, Martha, continued to spoil him with food and drink and care.

Within one day after they arrived at the yard, Linus Raines disappeared. Hawkstone never saw him again. Martha did not appear to miss the deserter. She dressed modest as a school teacher. She was tiny, with cute chubby cheeks, glistening raven black hair, and her father's deep mahogany eyes. She had a chirpy, bubbly personality, and, thankfully for Hawkstone, she did not baby-talk to her infant girl, Suzy. She brought Hawkstone his food, and assisted the nurse in changing bandages, and walked with him along the docks, sometimes bringing little Suzy. But Hawkstone spent little time in a bed. He was interested in the ships, and closely watched their construction until Captain Ben Coral returned from Seattle. Martha had told Hawkstone that was where Raines had been taken.

Hawkstone was in the boatyard shack where he lived, writing Rachel another letter, when Ben Coral roared through the open doorway with a bottle of Jamaican rum. Rain pounded against the window looking out over the wet fir skeleton of a partially completed clipper. Ben slammed

146

the door shut, pulled off his wool coat, and dragged up a chair opposite Hawkstone.

'Everything is set. The *Swordfish* has sailed from Seattle bound for the Horn and across the Atlantic to Gibraltar. She will cross the Strait to Morocco and deliver her passenger. My good friend Hausa, a Berber who was educated here in San Francisco, is a scout for Sahara caravans and deals in the selling and buying of camels. He will escort the passenger to Marrakech to meet the slave caravan bound southwest to the Niger, then north to Timbuktu and the slave auction.' He poured both glasses full, then downed half his in one swallow. 'Am I going too fast for you, my friend?'

Hawkstone swallowed the clawing sweet rum. 'How does Martha feel about all this?'

Ben nodded. 'She has read the report I ordered on the activities of Linus Raines up until you dumped him in my office. She accepts the divorce and feels the future laid out for him is just. Besides. . . .'

Hawkstone leaned back. 'She has found somebody else.'

'Ah, she has. A seaman called Swinging Jack McCall, a young Irish lad who fought his way through taverns and bars and landed a berth as common seaman, then worked his way, self-motivated, to read and write and navigate his way over the rails to bo'sun, then third mate on deck. He knows the sea, and he worships my little Martha and idolizes tiny Suzy, so he's a good match to bring into my brood. Martha is still a little in awe of him. He's big as you and me, and to the world outside he's a bit rough, but he's got a glint in his eye and a chiselled-rock jaw, and the respect of men around him.'

Ben finished off the glass of Jamaican rum and poured himself another. He topped off Hawkstone's glass. 'I see a wedding ahead. Martha and Swinging Jack will command the *Swordfish*. They will co-command with him listed as Captain and she as First Mate. My little Martha knows much about ships at sea, but history is still too young to accept a woman as Captain of a seagoing vessel. Times are changing, and if women and blacks and the oppressed are patient, if they educate themselves without shouting and screeching and screaming demands, they will eventually get what they want. History will see to it.' He squinted out of the rain-splattered window. 'My little girl will command her own ship one day, mark my words. Maybe not the *Swordfish*, but a ship just as fine and just as big.'

Hawkstone worked his healing muscles, about ready for travel. He pursed his lips and took another swallow. 'But the *Swordfish* will be in Morocco.'

'Aye, she will. The loving young couple will have to be sailed there to take command.' Ben pointed to the glistening wet skeleton outside the window. 'That is the ship that will take them, along with hauling a cargo of lumber to the South China Sea in exchange for silks and tea, and pearls from the Sea of Japan. She will accumulate gold and diamonds along the coast of Africa, and after her call at Morocco, visit the interesting ports of Europe along the skirts of the Mediterranean from the coast of Spain to Greek Isles.' Ben sat back with the glass in his hand. 'If she was your ship, Anson, what would be her name?'

Hawkstone blinked with surprise. 'Now, hold your draw just a minute, Ben.'

Ben leaned forward. 'I can see by the shine in your eyes you ain't against the idea. You got to convince Rachel is all. She will have to be with you. I give you that task.' He smiled, looking out of the window. 'Be good to see her, get a hug from her. As I recall she gave damn fine hugs.' He slapped his hand on the table. 'You leave tomorrow or the day after for Arizona Territory. I know you don't like train travel. Your buckskin and mule have been well fed and watered and exercised. They are ready. You've healed enough for the ride. You get that woman in her hut and you make her smile and you sweet-talk her to a life at sea.'

'I'd never go without her.'

'Then think on a name for the ship.'

'I don't have to. If this comes to be, the name would be easy. I'd want her called the *Rachel Cleary*.'

'And that she will be,' Captain Ben Coral said.

TWENTY-NINE

A sunset cold wind blew across mesquite and sage as Hawkstone approached the Apache village hut. He walked the buckskin with the packed mule in tow. In addition to goods, the pack carried twenty-five thousand in gold coin packed by Captain Ben Coral himself. But because Hawkstone had pushed himself from impatience, the long trail stirred healing wounds. He felt drained and weary, but he knew rest with her waited ahead. More than rest, intimate conversation and her touch was there for him.

As the buckskin walked closer to the hut and village, he saw her sitting in the setting sun, the clay pipe in her hand, leaning forward watching him come, her red hair bright in scarlet-slipping sunlight.

She did not run to him like a young girl with foolish romantic notions. She stood. She put the pipe on the chair he had built and placed beside hers. She tossed her long red hair back over her shoulders and took ten steps towards him, her smile showing she was happy to have him back.

When the buckskin was next to her, she said, 'Swing on down and get yourself close to me where you belong.'

He stepped out of the saddle and she was in his arms pushing close, kissing his neck, working along his jaw to find his mouth which she moulded with hers, with no attempt to hide her eagerness.

'You feel good, woman,' he said.

She kissed him again. 'I'll show you more inside.'

'I got to tend to the animals.'

'I'll help you unpack, then you got to tend to me. It's been too long. We got business together, you and me.'

'Yes'm, we surely do,' he said. He kissed her again.

Rachel Good Squaw, the medicine woman, did not see patients for the next two days. Hawkstone felt washed with the warmth of her loving attention. With her on her pinto and he on the buckskin, they rode to the river and sat on the bank and talked. He told her all of it, the months that had passed and the people he had met. They walked hand-in-hand along the water flow, and found a place to strip naked and swim, then make love.

Lying on the bank in afternoon sun, entwined, their clothes next to them, she said, 'You was gone too long, Anson. I don't want you away that long again. The ache is too strong.'

It was then he told her about a ship called the *Rachel Cleary*, and a possible life at sea.

She listened with her eyes closed, her red hair still wet, her long slender leg over his bullet-scarred limbs, forehead touching his. With a break in the talk, she was silent for a full minute. 'Is a life at sea what you want?'

'From the Pacific to the Atlantic to the South China Sea; from the Solomon Islands to Madagascar; from Tasmania to Morocco to the Greek Isles, I've seen the ports and mingled with the people. But the world has changed since those days. I was much younger, and mostly alone, except for Ben. Yes, a life at sea, but only if you are by my side. None of it will work for me if you ain't there.'

'You left me to go to sea once. If I say no, will you go without me?'

'Never,' he said. 'I only leave you at all 'cause you get

151

weary of my company.'

She lightly punched his shoulder. 'I sure ain't weary of it now. Mebbe I will be again, but not any time soon.'

He kissed her, always enjoying the taste of her lips. 'Woman, you have been the great love of my life since you was sixteen. I lost you and found you and I ain't ever going to be without you in my life.'

'Don't leave me as long as you did.'

'No. Your skin feels cold. We better get dressed.'

She rolled over on him and kissed him again. 'Not jest yet.'

At night they sat in the two chairs outside her hut. He smoked his rolled cigarettes, she her clay pipe. Some nights they drank tea, others they shared a whiskey bottle while they watched the star-dusted sky, and the moon when it filled. She told him she would think on the *Rachel Cleary*. She allowed as how she had never lived anywhere but Indian villages since she was sixteen and was driven from the orphanage. She wasn't sure how she would take to the sea. She was the medicine woman for the village. To give that up might be too long a stretch. Her answer would come soon. For now, she just wanted to enjoy him and his company.

She held his hand. 'You're the only man I could possibly love, you know that Anson Hawkstone.'

'Yes.'

'For me there will never be another.'

He placed his hand on her leg. 'My life with you is everything I want.'

'Give me a Ben Franklyn,' she whispered.

He sat with his mind searching. '*A good woman and health are a man's best wealth.*'

She leaned to his chair and kissed him well.

He felt home, yet with Rachel by his side he would always be home, wherever they were together, land or sea.

After a long silence, she said, 'What became of the outlaw,

Linus Raines?'

Hawkstone flipped his spent smoke into the desert. 'Ben said he'd write about what happened. Last I heard, Raines was delivered to a caravan scout somewhere in Morocco.'

THIRTY

Linus Raines understood none of it. The noisy lizard-face woman kept whipping his back with her leather quirt that looked like something from an old Southern plantation before the war. Nothing he did pleased her. She spoke not one word of English. During the voyage to Gibraltar aboard the *Swordfish*, Captain Thomas did not treat him like a guest, an important guest, the son-in-law of the shipyard owner, Captain Ben Coral. Linus did not share the captain's table. He ate in the general mess with common seamen. His complaints were ignored by all. It had been a rough passage round the Horn and across the Atlantic.

And where was his sweet wife, Martha?

Once he walked off the gangplank in Morocco, he was grabbed by heavily draped natives and dragged to their camp. It was there that he met the man Hausa, the only human around him to speak English. Only his deep pools of dark brown eyes showed out of what Linus learned was a tuareg. Hausa sat opposite Linus in the camp and sipped his tiny glass of tea taken from enamel pots. None was offered to Linus. To a sing-song wail, all others touched head to ground in prayer.

'Can I have some tea?' he asked. 'And food. I need something to eat.'

'Allah will provide,' Hausa said.

'I got nothing to do with Allah. Get me something to eat.'
Linus frowned. 'When does all that noisy wailing stop?'

He received no answer. Hausa sat with only his eyes and
the dark skin around them showing in the campfire. The
night was black, with little local light coming from the fire.
'It will end soon. You will eat when it is decided.'

'What does that mean?'

Hausa sipped. 'You are not a person. You have no name,
no demands or wishes. Madagu is the caravan chief. He is
your master. For all purpose, he is your god. The lizard-face,
Noisy Woman, assigns your chores. You will obey her without
question, or she will whip you.'

Linus squinted at him, his heart pounding. 'What are you
saying?'

'I say, your name is Slave. The caravan marches forty-
three slaves, you are but one. I am the scout. I am Berber
and I provide the camels. In the morning, the caravan
travels to Marrakech where we pick up twenty more slaves
from Khartoum and add them for the long journey to
Timbuktu and the slave auction. The African black Bantu
are shipped across the sea to America. It is coming to the
time for religious human sacrifice. Many will die along the
way, but Timbuktu provides human sacrifice slaves, the most
prized being those with white skin. Since the eleventh
century millions of slaves have walked the trail. White skin
slaves are now rare, not many Christians taken these days
since Barbary pirates stopped raiding the coasts. You will be
popular.'

The wailing ended. Carpets were rolled as believers stood.

Linus thought he was going to faint. 'I can't be a slave. It
isn't possible.'

'Ah, not only possible, but real.'

Sheep bleated around Linus. Camels made a sound like
gargling and snapped at anyone who walked by, and other
camels. Voices cackled in a language he did not understand.

Since Hausa alone spoke English, only Hausa could help him escape the nightmare lunacy that could not be happening.

'I'm an American,' Linus croaked. 'You can't do this to me.'

Hausa nodded. 'Ah, yes, an American. When the Bantu blacks go to America they say they are African and do not belong there. Black voices fall on deaf American ears. You once were an American. Now you are Slave, and you will travel to Timbuktu where you will be auctioned. You will obey Noisy Woman, the woman with the wrinkled face, or she will whip you until you bleed raw.'

'But . . . I can't understand anyone. How can I know what she's saying?'

'I will interpret. I promised my friend, Captain Ben Coral, I would do that.'

Linus sat stiff. 'What? You promised, what? But . . . I have a wife, a child. This ain't happening. It can't.'

Hausa finished his tea and immediately washed and dried the glass and placed it in a small wooden case. 'No wife. No child. You have been divorced from them. They have another now. You are only Slave, nothing else. You will be auctioned in Timbuktu if you are still alive.'

Linus churned inside with fear and dread. 'I can't be a slave.'

'Of course you can. It is as certain as we sit here in the dark Sahara night preparing for our journey to Marrakech. You will grow used to your new life, Slave.'

Linus Raines was tied with his hands in front connected to the long line of other slaves. They trudged behind the camel caravan along a hot Sahara unmarked trail. Hausa led the way on his own camel, followed by twenty-two others. All Linus learned came from Hausa, the only man he understood. Talking went on constantly all around him, even among other slaves. He understood none of it.

When camp was set up, a large tent was erected for Madagu and his four women. As caravan leader he was unapproachable to a slave. Visitors went in and out of his tent. Hausa was one of them. Linus was busy in camp getting camel fodder cut from coarse plants and left by others for him and other slaves to gather. He would not be trusted with a knife. When they reached the occasional oasis, he picked palm fronds to be braided to ropes.

Everybody talked, some barking orders, others just making noise. Even the camels voiced opinions. He noticed that the camel Hausa rode, and the three towed behind him, had their flanks shaven and were tattooed. After gathering the fodder, he was given a bowl of millet porridge mixed with spicy herbal sauce and a cup of camel milk to drink. Every day at sunset the wailing and praying carried across the Sahara. A few nights everybody ate camel meat, the unworthy parts going to unworthy slaves. After eating, Slave was told to pick up camel chips for camp fires. If he did not have enough, Noisy Woman beat his back with her leather quirt. He yelped his complaints and once thought to yank the quirt away from her. He told this to Hausa one night on the trail as they sat in the sand with camel and voice noise barking around them.

Hausa said, 'Do not, Slave. It would be a serious crime for you to touch Noisy Woman.'

'She has to stop beating me. My back is raw.'

'Work harder.'

'I'm half starved, I can't stand that porridge.'

'Learn to like it.'

'Hausa, you got to help me bust loose from this bunch.'

In firelight, the liquid brown pool eyes narrowed from the slit in the Tuareg. 'We carry the white gold – a ton of salt, and real gold dust, and you can see the sheep. We also have strips of cotton cloth, kola nuts, glass beads, but mostly it is

157

salt for sale and trade. It preserves the meat and flavours food and is used for many other things. I must scout the way, I cannot help you escape. Escape to where? We are in the Sahara. To find the way I must study the stars, follow wind patterns, sand-dune formations, even during the day watch sand colour changes. I am burdened with much responsibility. The Sahara is in constant movement. There is nowhere for you to escape. Accept your fate, Slave, and work harder.'

Along the Bilma Trail as the caravan approached the Nile, they stopped for three days in the large Bilma Oasis, where some trade went on from outsiders. Hausa was too busy visiting to talk with Linus. Linus still had his chores, and when Noisy Woman saw his pathetic gathering of fronds, she whipped her quirt across his back. Too many blows for too long. Linus yelped, then gritted his teeth. Seeing his one chance for possible escape, he turned on her, and yanked the quirt away. He whacked it across her lizard face and was immediately grabbed and pushed to the sand by five burly men.

A stake had been driven into the sand. Linus was tied to it. His heart pounded because Noisy Woman and Hausa were in the tent with the caravan leader, Madagu. He knew they were deciding his fate. The lizard-face woman had repeatedly shouted the word, 'Die!' while pointing a bony finger at him. She had her quirt back in her hand when she entered the tent. Linus felt a wrenching pain in his stomach, partly from hunger, partly from fear.

At last in darkness Hausa came to him, his eyes showing relief and joy. 'Allah be praised, Slave, you will not die.'

Linus collapsed to sit on the sand, the relief taking the strength from his legs. He waited for his breathing to return to normal. 'Am I still a slave?'

'You will be slave the rest of your life. Noisy Woman had to be given something for punishment.'

'Punishment?'

'You touched her with your unworthy slave hands. And you took her prized possession. She demanded your blindness.'

'What?'

'Ah, but Allah be praised, she told us she would settle for a hand.'

'What?'

'It was explained to her that you needed your sight and your hands to do the work. So, thanks be to Allah, she will only require your left foot.'

Linus felt conscious thinking leave him.

A month later the caravan had reached Timbuktu and the slaves were bunched together in a large corral. Linus Raines covered his nose from the smell. He wore a cotton robe draped over his head and reaching to his ankles – his one ankle. Where his left foot had been was still not completely healed. And the pain, he still felt the pain.

Hausa came to him and drew him, hopping, to the edge of the slaves. 'Slave, this is the last time I will see you.'

Linus felt his chest turn hollow. 'But I don't understand these people. I can only talk to you.'

'No longer matters. The circle has been closed.' He stood with his hands crossed in front of him, the chocolate pools of his eyes without expression. 'You will not go on the block. The fanatics have made their bid for religious human sacrifice, and have already purchased you.'

Linus felt all blood leave his face and skin. Tingling crossed his forehead. 'What are you saying?'

'There was some problem. Their beliefs require the whole human for the sacrifice. You, of course, have a missing foot. But Allah be praised, the wrinkled-face woman kept your foot after the axe separated it, wrapped in cloth. She will present it with you as a package. My debt has now been paid.'

Linus, with a tingling head and beginning to shiver despite the heat, said, 'Debt? Debt?'

'Yes, my debt for my education to Captain Ben Coral. With you now to become a religious sacrifice, the circle is complete. Bringing you here for this purpose closes the ends and completes my debt to the captain.'

'Please,' Linus croaked.

Hausa stepped back as four men dressed like monks came up behind him and reached for Linus. Hausa said, 'You must have done something very bad against the captain, Linus Raines. Good-bye, one-time husband to Captain Ben Coral's beautiful daughter. You belong to Allah now.'

between the two guns, the Peacemaker aimed directly at Raines' face.

'Empty your hand,' he said.

Raines looked at Hawkstone harsh. 'He ain't gonna shoot me down like a dog.'

'No, he ain't,' Hawkstone said.

'Out of the way, Hawkstone,' Brag said.

Raines squinted and stared without recognition. 'Who the hell are you?'

Hawkstone eased the buckskin alongside Raines and jerked the Colt from his hand and pushed it in his waistband. 'Sit easy. It ain't important you know me.' He looked back over his shoulder at Brag. 'Put it away.' He leaned toward Lindsey. 'You still with us, girl?'

Lindsey gave him a curt nod. She shook her head to move some of the hair off her face. Her hands remained tied to the saddle horn. She stared at Raines with defiant hate.

Raines chuckled with a grin. 'A misunderstanding, fellas. If it's money you gents want, I got plenty.'

'I'll just bet you do,' Hawkstone said. He reached for and yanked the reins from Raines.

Brag holstered his Colt, as though he had decided to go along with Hawkstone. He moved the roan enough to reach out and untie Lindsey's hands. While she rubbed her wrists and brushed hair from her face, he turned to Hawkstone. 'What's your intent?'

Two crows cawed a loud complaint from a fir branch at the edge of the clearing.

Hawkstone said to Brag, 'After I hog-tie this cockroach, I'm riding him to Soda Springs and wait for the wagon train so Lindsey will be safe. Then I'm hauling the bastard to San Francisco. You're welcome to ride along any part of that.'

Lindsey picked up her reins. 'You don't have to look after me. I can take care of myself.'

Hawkstone glared at her. 'Hush yourself up, young lady. I

kicking up a fuss, giving him a lot of bother in his kidnap-
ping hopes. But what did Hawkstone know about the
thinking of a twenty-two-year-old female mind? Nothing.
Might be she succumbed once again to his boyish charm,
and was giving him everything he wanted from her.

Coming daylight made trail-following easier. The sky
lightened, though puffy grey clouds eased in over the mountain tops. The forest thickened, though rocky canyons and
passes still dominated.

Brag was the first to see them. He and Hawkstone topped
a ridge and he silently pointed through sparse skinny pines
along a draw. Raines led the way with Lindsey on a brown
behind him. Her wrists were tied to the saddle horn. She
wore no bonnet and her blonde hair strung straggled
enough to hide her young face. He had his hands full following the thin trail while holding her reins. Brag cleared
his holster. He urged the roan towards the draw as he
cocked the hammer on his Colt.

Hawkstone moved beside him and put his hand on Brag's
gun arm. Brag pushed the arm away and rode forwards. The
draw ended on a flat clearing the size of a small corral.
Raines turned when he heard the saddle and reins creak
and jingle as Brag's roan stiffened his front legs to brace
himself when he reached the clearing. Raines dropped
Lindsey's reins and reached for his Colt.

Brag shouted, 'Drop it or I'll shoot you out of the saddle!'
Hawkstone reached the clearing ten seconds after Brag.
Lindsey shrank in the saddle and stared at the two
approaching men. Her blue eyes were without life. Her
horse eased back from the sorrel.

Hawkstone saw the scene freeze around him. Somehow
he had to get himself between Raines and Brag. Raines had
just cleared his holster. His eyes became slits. Hawkstone
bumped his buckskin into Brag's roan as he drew his
Peacemaker. Brag's Colt wavered. Hawkstone moved